There's trouble in the Sunset Farm's corral.

MICHELLE

Michelle loves her riding lessons at the Sunset Farm Stables. She's made friends with everyone who works there—including the horses.

But when Michelle finds out that her favorite horse, Chestnut, is being sold—and sent to New York City, she knows she has to do something. New York City is no place for a little horse like Chestnut! She has to hide him—and hope that no one finds him. Including her older sister, Stephanie.

STEPHANIE

Stephanie nearly freaked when she found out her major crush, Jack, volunteered at the same stable where Michelle took her riding lessons. To get a little closer to Jack, Stephanie volunteered there, too.

Now, a horse, Chestnut, is missing at the stable. Stephanie knows it would totally impress Jack if she found the little foal. And that's exactly what she intends to do.

FULL HOUSE™ SISTERS books

Two on the Town
One Boss Too Many
And the Winner Is . . .
How to Hide a Horse
Problems in Paradise
   (coming in December)

Available from MINSTREL Books

FULL HOUSE™
Sisters

How to Hide a Horse

ELIZABETH WINFREY

A Parachute Book

Published by POCKET BOOKS

New York   London   Toronto   Sydney   Singapore

This book is a work of fiction. Names, characters, places and incidents are products of the author's imagination or are used fictitiously. Any resemblance to actual events or locales or persons living or dead is entirely coincidental.

A MINSTREL PAPERBACK *Original*

A Minstrel Book published by
POCKET BOOKS, a division of Simon & Schuster Inc.
1230 Avenue of the Americas, New York, NY 10020

A PARACHUTE PRESS BOOK

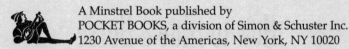

Copyright © and ™ 1999 by Warner Bros.

FULL HOUSE, characters, names and all related indicia are trademarks of Warner Bros. © 1999.

ISBN: 0-671-04056-1

First Minstrel Books printing November 1999

10 9 8 7 6 5 4 3 2 1

A MINSTREL BOOK and colophon are registered trademarks of Simon & Schuster Inc.

Printed in the U.S.A.

MICHELLE

Chapter
1

Faster, Clancy, faster!" Michelle Tanner urged. She pressed her knees against the gentle black mare. Her blond hair blew out from under her hat as the horse trotted faster.

"Yahoo!" Michelle exclaimed. She shaded her blue eyes with one hand and grinned at her two best friends, Mandy Metz and Cassie Wilkins, as she passed them.

"We're like real cowgirls!" Mandy called. "Go, Buttercup!" Mandy's dark, curly ponytail bounced up and down as the horse she rode trotted forward.

On the other side of the corral, the girls' riding instructor, Sabrina Hutchinson, waved. "Hey, Michelle," she called. "Great form!"

"Whoa, girl." Michelle pulled carefully on her reins, and Clancy slowed to a walk. Michelle smiled. Her western-style horseback riding lessons were really paying off. Every day she was getting better and better. Soon, she hoped, she would be one of the best riders at Sunset Farm.

Michelle took a deep breath of fresh air. Yes, Sunset Farm was her new favorite place. The stables were just ten minutes from where Michelle lived in San Francisco, but it felt as if they were on a whole different planet. There was no traffic or noise there.

Instead, there was a large fenced-in area called a corral, where Michelle and her friends practiced their riding. Then there was the big barn with stalls for each horse. Plus, everywhere there were green pastures where the horses exercised and munched on the grass in the bright afternoon sun.

In the two months she'd been taking lessons at the stable, Michelle had gotten to know the personalities of all the horses. Clancy was gentle and kind. Lightning was beautiful but a little wild. Amazon was lively, and Beauty would do practically anything for a carrot or a lump of sugar.

"Clancy really likes you," Cassie said to Michelle. She brushed her sand-colored hair out of her eyes and reached down to pet her horse, Amazon. "Too bad Amazon doesn't listen to what I say."

"Don't worry," Michelle assured her friend. "After you have a few more lessons, you'll be able to get Amazon to walk, trot, or gallop whenever you want."

"That's all for today, girls," Sabrina called. "Bring the horses in. You're all looking terrific out there!"

Michelle patted Clancy's neck as they headed toward the barn entrance. She heard the neighs and whinnies of the horses inside. Michelle chuckled to herself. There were so many horses living in the barn, it was almost as full as *her* house.

Michelle's dad, Danny, lived in the house along with Michelle's sisters, thirteen-year-old Stephanie and eighteen-year-old D.J.

3

Then there was the rest of the family.

When Michelle was a baby and her mom died, Danny needed help taking care of his three daughters. So Danny asked his best friend, Joey Gladstone, and Michelle's Uncle Jesse to move in with them. It was totally cool having *three* dads!

Then Uncle Jesse met and married Becky Donaldson. A few years later they had twin boys, Nicky and Alex, who were five years old now. Last but not least, there was the family's golden retriever, Comet.

Talk about a full house!

"Whoa, Clancy, whoa." Michelle pulled back on the horse's reins. Clancy stopped in front of Sabrina. "Good girl."

Sabrina held the reins as Michelle threw her leg over the horse's back and hopped to the ground. "Can I give Clancy a carrot or a lump of sugar?" she asked the riding instructor.

"Of course." Sabrina smiled as she glanced at Clancy.

"Here's some, Michelle!" Annie Montgomery called from her perch on the corral fence. "I've got a whole pocket full of sugar."

"Excellent!" Mandy exclaimed. "Sugar! The horses are going to *love* us if we give them some of that." She slipped off Buttercup and jogged over to Michelle.

Cassie joined them, walking gingerly. "That's it. I'm officially saddle sore." She frowned.

Michelle smiled. So far, Cassie didn't love riding as much as Michelle and Mandy did.

"Hey, guys," Annie greeted them. "How's it going?"

As always, Annie was wearing a pair of faded jeans and dusty black cowboy boots. Her wildly curly red hair peeked out from under her cowboy hat.

Annie's father, Mr. Montgomery, owned Sunset Farm. The three girls had become good friends with Annie when they started riding lessons.

Annie was one of the most adventurous girls Michelle had ever met. She wasn't afraid of *anything*. Michelle had even seen Annie make six-foot jumps on her horse. Plus she knew more about Sunset Farm than the most experienced volunteers at the stable.

"Hi, Annie," Michelle said as she walked up to her friend. She took a sugar cube from Annie to give to Clancy. Then she slipped another one into the pocket of her jeans. She was saving it for another, very special horse.

Annie jumped off the wooden fence and handed sugar cubes to Mandy and Cassie. The girls walked back to Clancy, Buttercup, and Amazon. Michelle held her hand under Clancy's mouth. She giggled as the mare nuzzled her palm.

"I'm saving a sugar cube for Chestnut," Michelle told Clancy.

Visiting Chestnut, Clancy's six-month-old foal, was Michelle's favorite part of the afternoon. Every time Michelle saw the little horse, she felt filled with love.

"Let's go see Chestnut now," Mandy suggested. She must have been reading Michelle's mind.

Annie nodded. "Sure."

The girls walked through the doors of the barn toward Chestnut's stall. Michelle eyed several short fences, the kind used to practice jumping, leaning against a wall.

"I can't wait until we learn to jump," Michelle said as the group headed past Lightning's stall. "That will be totally cool."

"Oh, sure," Cassie agreed. "That will be great. The wind in my hair, the sun in my face, the sound of me hitting the ground—"

"We get the idea, Cass. No jumping for you." Michelle laughed.

She breathed deeply. She loved the scent of the barn. In fact, Michelle loved *everything* about the barn. She glanced around at the row of stalls, each stall with a horse's name on it. There were always at least a dozen people around. Some groomed horses while others mucked out the stalls or repaired saddles.

"Hey there, Michelle!" a man called.

Michelle turned and saw a man older than her father with thick white hair. He was wearing blue jeans, a T-shirt, and a denim jacket. "Joe! What's up?"

Joe was Michelle's favorite stable hand. He was always giving her pointers about riding, and he always had a smile for her—and a carrot for her favorite foal.

"Off to give Chestnut a snack?" Joe asked.

7

"Yup!" Michelle answered. "I've got it right here." She held up the sugar cube. Immediately a whinny sounded from behind her.

"Hi, Chestnut." Michelle turned and stepped up to one of the stalls.

Clancy's foal, Chestnut, stood inside. He was the most beautiful horse Michelle had ever seen. His coat was brown and shiny, and his giant eyes were such a dark brown, they were almost black.

As soon as he saw Michelle, Chestnut shook his mane from side to side and nickered softly. Michelle laughed with delight.

"I'm happy to see you, too, Chestnut. Do you want some sugar?" Michelle held out the lump.

The tiny horse stretched his neck toward Michelle, his eyes shining brightly. Michelle felt a wave of pure love as she fed Chestnut the sugar.

Cassie, Mandy, and Annie stood beside Michelle, cooing over the little horse and petting his mane.

"No doubt about it," Annie said. "You and Chestnut are true-blue pals, Michelle."

Michelle filled with pride. She had been in the stable when Chestnut was born. As soon as she saw the foal's deep brown coat, Michelle suggested the name Chestnut. Mr. Montgomery agreed that it was the perfect name for the newborn horse.

Ever since that afternoon Michelle and Chestnut's bond had grown every day. It was almost as if Chestnut were Michelle's own colt.

"Good, boy," Michelle murmured. "Yum, yum." Chestnut stared right into Michelle's eyes as she spoke. He seemed to understand every word.

Michelle turned to Annie. "I can't wait until Chestnut gets big and strong enough to ride," she said. "I'm going to teach him everything. We'll be a great team."

"Yeah," Annie agreed, her voice so soft it was almost a whisper.

Michelle frowned as she studied Annie's face. Her friend looked totally sad.

"What's wrong?" Michelle asked. "You look like you just lost your best friend."

"I feel like I'm about to," Annie answered.

"What is it, Annie?" Cassie asked. "You can tell us."

Annie glanced from Chestnut to the three girls. "Well, I overheard my dad talking on the phone this morning."

"And?" Mandy urged. "What did he say?"

"He's selling some of the horses—Chestnut may be one of them." Annie bit her lip as she waited for the bad news to sink in.

"Oh, no!" Michelle moaned. Chestnut couldn't be sold. He just couldn't. Michelle loved him too much.

I have to save Chestnut, Michelle told herself. *I have to stop Mr. Montgomery before it's too late!*

Chapter
2

❚s pepperoni one of the four basic food groups?" Stephanie Tanner wondered out loud. She was flipping through her *Teen Trends* magazine as she snagged a slice of pie at Anthony's Pizzeria.

"If it's not, it should be," Allie Taylor answered. "I don't think I could go more than two days without eating Anthony's pepperoni pizza."

Stephanie took a huge bite of her slice. "I have to eat fast," she told her best friend. "I'm leaving in a few minutes to pick up Michelle at her riding lesson."

"Thrilling," Allie commented. "A half hour

ride on the bus is almost as exciting as a trip to the dentist."

Stephanie smiled. Allie was an only child. She never understood what it was like to have to do a favor for a sister.

"You should smell Michelle after one of her lessons," Stephanie told her. "She might as well be a horse herself. I've been thinking about buying a nose plug."

Allie laughed and took a huge gulp of soda. "Well, before you leave, let's talk about the dance."

Yes! The John Muir Middle School dance. Stephanie had been thinking of it almost non-stop for the past several days. She simply had to have a date for the big event. And she knew just who she wanted the lucky guy to be. Now, if she could only get him to ask her. . . .

"Do you think Charlie is going to ask me?" Allie blurted out. "He hasn't said a word about it yet."

Allie had spent the past two months hoping that she and her debate partner, Charlie Rubin, would form a relationship based on more than carefully planned arguments.

So far, though, Charlie seemed more interested in looking at index cards than in gazing into Allie's eyes.

Which is why she and Stephanie decided to look for help in *Teen Trends* magazine. Stephanie glanced down at the article she was reading. "Getting Your Dream Date: 25 Pointers for Snagging Your Perfect Guy."

"According to this," Stephanie reported, "you should be 'open, warm, and friendly, and smile your biggest smile. It's a sure way to send Mr. Right the right signal.' "

Allie groaned. "I've tried that—and Charlie *still* hasn't gotten the picture."

Stephanie shrugged. "The dance is two weeks away. In boy time, that's, like, a year and a half. Charlie probably thinks he's got plenty of time left. Give him a few more days."

"Good idea," Allie agreed. "Maybe I should drop some hints while Charlie and I are preparing for our next debate."

Stephanie laughed. "Like point number one: Charlie Rubin should ask Allie Taylor to the big dance—*now.*"

Allie blushed pink. "I think I could be a *bit* more subtle than that, Steph."

"I did it!" a familiar voice yelled.

Allie and Stephanie turned at the same time. Darcy Powell bounded over to their booth, her dark eyes gleaming with excitement. "Hey, guys! I did it!"

"Congratulations!" Stephanie said. She paused. "Uh, what did you do exactly?"

Darcy grinned as she slid into the booth beside Allie. Her smooth dark skin was flushed. "I asked Troy Allman to the dance!"

"No way!" Allie exclaimed. "You didn't!"

"What did he say?" Stephanie asked, leaning forward. This was some seriously juicy information.

Darcy wiggled her dark eyebrows. "He said *yes!*"

"Nice!" Stephanie reached across the table and gave Darcy a high-five.

"Thank you, thank you. I'll be signing autographs outside Anthony's later today," Darcy joked.

Allie sat there with her mouth hanging open. "I can't believe it," she finally said. "I can't believe you asked one of the cutest football players at John Muir to the dance!"

Stephanie had to laugh. Darcy and Allie were such opposites. Ever since Stephanie had met Allie her first year in school, her friend had been shy and quiet. Darcy, on the other hand had been totally outgoing since she moved to San Francisco in the fourth grade.

"Hey, no guts no glory. Right?" Darcy asked.

"Right!" Stephanie agreed. "You rule, Darce."

Out of the corner of her eye, Stephanie caught a flash of denim and flannel. A very *cute* flash.

"Hello, Earth to Stephanie! Who are you staring at?" Allie asked. "Your jaw is practically in the pizza."

Stephanie blinked. Oops. She *had* been staring. "Over there. It's Jack O'Shea," she whispered loudly.

"If you keep staring at him like that, he's going to think he has pizza sauce on his face," Darcy commented.

Stephanie tore her gaze away from Jack, who had stepped up to the To Go counter. She felt her face getting red just from looking at him.

"I would give *anything* to go to the dance

with Jack," Stephanie said with a sigh. She had had a crush on him for weeks now. He had jet-black hair and the brightest blue eyes Stephanie had ever seen.

"So go for it," Darcy urged. "Ask him to the dance."

Stephanie shook her head. "No. I can't. No way."

She could barely bring herself to speak to Jack, much less ask him to a dance. Not that she didn't want to.

Every morning she walked into history class determined to ask Jack if she could borrow a pencil at least. Every morning she wimped out. Which really wasn't like her. There was just something about Jack that made her all nervous inside.

"At least you know he doesn't have a girlfriend," Allie pointed out. "*Yet.*"

As soon as Stephanie had confessed her latest crush to Allie and Darcy, her best friends had checked around. According to everyone they asked, Jack wasn't going out with anyone.

Stephanie still had doubts. How could a guy as cute and nice as Jack *not* have a girlfriend?

"I just get so stupid around him," Stephanie said. "Every time I walk past his desk, I manage either to drop a book or trip over my feet."

"You're going to have to get over that," Allie teased. "Otherwise, you're going to injure yourself seriously on the night of the dance."

"Don't worry, I have a plan," Stephanie announced. "First, I get him to like me. *Then* I get him to ask me to the dance. And this magazine article is going to show me how to do it."

She glanced back down at her article. "Getting Your Dream Date, pointer number two: Show your dream guy that you and he share common interests. Ones you'll be able to talk about on long, romantic dates."

"You'd better get moving, Steph." Darcy pointed at Stephanie with a piece of pizza. "The dance is only two weeks away."

Stephanie gulped. Darcy was right. If she wanted Jack to be her date—and she *did*—then she was going to have to come up with a plan. *Pronto.*

MICHELLE

Chapter 3

Michelle frowned. She stared into Chestnut's deep brown eyes. She still couldn't believe what Annie had just said. Was Mr. Montgomery really going to sell the little horse? Sunset Farm wouldn't be the same without him.

"Hey, Michelle." Cassie said, breaking into Michelle's thoughts. "Mandy, Annie, and I are going out back to play with the rabbits. Why don't you come?"

"I'll be there in a couple of minutes," Michelle answered. She wanted to spend more time with Chestnut before Stephanie came to take her home.

She stroked the little horse's mane. He nuzzled her with his soft, velvety nose.

"Oh, Chestnut, there must be something I can do to keep you here," Michelle moaned. "But what?"

Michelle glanced over her shoulder. She could see Annie's dad talking on the phone in his office, through a half-open door across the barn.

"I have to ask if it's really true," Michelle told Chestnut. "I have to ask Mr. Montgomery if he's really sending you away."

She headed toward the office. If Mr. Montgomery really were selling Chestnut, Michelle thought, maybe she could talk him out of it.

I'll just explain that Chestnut belongs here at Sunset Farm, Michelle decided. *Once he hears what I have to say, Mr. Montgomery will definitely change his mind.*

Michelle stopped a few steps before Mr. Montgomery's office to prepare her speech. *I'm here to beg you to keep Chestnut,* she might say. Sure. Why not? There was nothing wrong with the direct approach.

Michelle lifted her right hand to knock on

the door. Before she had a chance to let Mr. Montgomery know she was there, he moved forward and closed the door.

She had missed her chance. Now what?

Michelle tapped her foot against the floor of the barn and considered her options. She could wait for Mr. Montgomery to come out of his office, then pounce. Or she could—

"I think that would be fine for Chestnut," she heard Mr. Montgomery say. "Yes, yes, thank you—"

She could crouch next to the door and spy through the old-fashioned keyhole.

Yes. That was definitely the best option. If Annie's dad was talking about Chestnut, Michelle wanted to know exactly what he was saying.

Unfortunately, at least half of Mr. Montgomery's words were drowned out by the sounds of horses neighing and stable hands working. Michelle crouched down and pressed her ear close to the keyhole.

"Yes, New York. I understand," Mr. Montgomery said.

New York? Why was he talking about New York? Michelle wondered.

"Uh-huh. That price is acceptable," Mr. Montgomery said. "Clancy and Chestnut will be ready to be shipped to New York in three days."

Three days! New York! Michelle's eyes widened.

"Thanks, Roger. And say hello to the Big Apple for me." Then Mr. Montgomery laughed at something the other man said.

"I'm looking forward to seeing you, too. Hey, why don't you bring me one of those black cowboy hats you're always wearing? Mine is getting a little worn." Mr. Montgomery laughed again. "Bye, Roger." Inside the office, Annie's dad hung up the telephone.

Michelle was stunned. Oh, no! Mr. Montgomery really *was* selling Chestnut and Clancy! Annie had been right.

The worst thing was, he was shipping the little foal to New York City!

Michelle had been to the Big Apple with her family, and she loved the city. It was exciting and full of interesting things to see. It was no place for a horse like Chestnut, though.

All of the horses Michelle had seen in New York pulled heavy carriages around Central Park. Poor Chestnut wasn't strong enough to handle that kind of work!

Even a grown-up mare like Clancy might choke on the pollution from the thousands of cars that crowded the city streets.

Michelle had to protect Chestnut. Otherwise, her favorite foal would get hurt—or worse.

She *had* to help Chestnut. Now she just needed to figure out how.

Crouching down, Michelle pressed her ear to the keyhole again. Maybe Mr. Montgomery would make another phone call. She had to get as much information about the sale of the horses as possible.

Now no sound came from inside the office at all. She pressed her ear closer.

Suddenly Michelle felt a hand on her shoulder. "Michelle! What are you doing?"

Yikes! She leapt three feet in the air, jumping as far away from the door as possible. She was caught! Caught snooping!

Michelle whipped her head around and found herself face-to-face with—her older sister.

"Uh—hi, Steph," Michelle said lamely.

Stephanie stared at Michelle, questioning her sister with her eyes.

"I guess I'll just tell Mandy and Cassie we're ready to go," Michelle said when her sister remained silent. "I'll be right back."

"Not so fast, little sister," Stephanie ordered. She gripped Michelle's shoulder. "We need to talk."

Uh-oh, Michelle thought. *Stephanie saw me spying. I'm totally busted!*

STEPHANIE

Chapter
4

Stephanie felt like hugging Michelle and giving her little sister a big kiss.

"I can't believe you were holding out on me! This is so awesome!" Stephanie whispered, and bounced up and down.

"Huh?" Michelle asked.

"Jack O'Shea. He's *here.*" Stephanie explained.

Who knew that Michelle's horseback riding lessons would lead me to the guy of my dreams? Stephanie thought.

Yes, it was true. None other than Jack O'Shea was standing not one hundred feet away.

Michelle frowned. "Jack O'Shea?" She paused. "You mean one of the guys who cleans out the stalls?"

"I mean Jack O'Shea, the cutest guy at John Muir Middle School," Stephanie said. "The guy I have a huge crush on. The guy I'm hoping will ask me to the biggest dance of the year!"

"Oh." Michelle stared at Stephanie with her round blue eyes. Clearly, she didn't understand just how big this was.

"How could you not tell me that he works here?" Stephanie whispered. She did *not* want Jack to overhear this particular conversation.

She glanced over her shoulder at Jack. He was at the far end of the barn now, looking just as amazing as he had when he walked into Anthony's forty-five minutes earlier.

Wow. Even with bits of hay stuck to his red plaid flannel shirt, Jack was the cutest guy Stephanie had ever seen.

Michelle raised her eyebrows. "How was I supposed to know you *liked* Jack, Steph," she pointed out. "I didn't even know you two knew each other!"

"Well, I *do* like him," Stephanie told her sis-

25

ter. "Even though we barely know each other. Now, tell me everything about him. What's he like? Does he work here every day? Does he ever talk about a girlfriend? Has he mentioned the dance?"

Michelle shrugged. "How should I know? It's not like I've ever really talked to him."

"Tell me *something*," Stephanie begged. "*Any*thing!"

"There's nothing to tell," Michelle answered. "He mucks out the stalls. He feeds the horses. That's all I know."

Stephanie sighed. It was confirmed. Little sisters had no idea what was truly important.

"Why don't you just walk over there and start a conversation?" Michelle suggested. "Then you can find out for yourself what kind of girl Jack likes."

Now, why didn't I think of that? Stephanie wondered. Not even a whole hour ago, Stephanie had promised herself that she was going to approach Jack and have an actual conversation with him. Now she had her chance, and she was wasting it by standing and grilling her little sister.

"Good idea, Michelle!" Stephanie said. "Thanks."

Michelle grinned. "I do what I can."

"Go hang out with Mandy and Cassie," Stephanie suggested. "I'll come find you in a few minutes." She shifted her weight from one foot to the other, too excited to stand still. "Yeah, I'll come get you right after I totally impress Jack and get him to ask me to the dance."

Stephanie pictured the whole scene happening just the way *Teen Trends* magazine suggested. She would casually walk up to Jack and start talking to him about horses. So what if she wasn't the world's foremost expert on riding? She could ask questions and that would show him they had a common interest. Maybe he'd ask her to the dance—or, at least, ask to spend more time with her.

Michelle raised her eyebrows. "Steph, you might want to be just a *little* less excited looking when you talk to Jack."

"Am I that obvious?" Stephanie asked.

Michelle nodded. "I don't know that much about boys, but I do think you should stop hopping around like that. Jack might think you're just the tiniest bit crazy. Or that you have to go to the bathroom."

"True." Stephanie took a deep breath and made sure she was standing still. "I'm totally calm and cool."

"Good luck." Michelle smiled. She turned and walked out of the barn.

Calm and cool, Stephanie repeated to herself. She took a few deep breaths, waiting for her pulse to get back to a normal rate. Then she put on a friendly smile and strolled toward Jack.

She stuck her hands into the pockets of her denim overalls to complete her casual look.

"Hi, Jack," Stephanie called. "Fancy meeting you here."

Ugh! She wanted to cry. That was a horrible, horrible line! What was this? One of Danny's favorite black-and-white movies? Stephanie wanted to shrink away and start over.

Wait—maybe Jack hadn't heard her. Maybe she could . . .

Jack glanced away from the pile of straw

that he was spreading out with a pitchfork. "Stephanie! Hey, what are you doing here?"

Whoops. Too late to back out now.

"Hi! I'm just—uh—picking up my little sister, Michelle," Stephanie offered.

"That's nice." Then silence. Jack stood there, staring at her.

Oh, no! Stephanie thought. This is going nowhere. *I have to think of something else to say!*

"She, uh, loves horses."

Ugh! Lame! Totally lame!

"So do I," Jack said. "I work here for free, just so I can ride the horses."

The line in *Teen Trends* found its way into her brain. *If you want to get a boy's attention, talk to him about his interests.*

"Uh, I love horses, too," Stephanie said. "And barns."

Jack inhaled deeply. "I know what you mean. Just the smell of this place makes me happy."

Stephanie sniffed the air. The scent was a combination of manure and sweat. Well, she couldn't say she *loved* the smell. "I can see how some would find it, uh, appealing."

Jack leaned his pitchfork against the door of the stall. He pulled half a carrot from the back pocket of his blue jeans. "Would you like to give this to Beauty?" he offered. "She'll be your best friend forever."

"Sure!" Stephanie took the carrot and held it toward Beauty's mouth.

Yikes! Stephanie jumped back—the horse's teeth were enormous, and sharp looking!

Jack chuckled. "Don't worry. She gets excited around carrots, but she's as gentle as a lamb."

"Worried? Not me." Stephanie flinched as Beauty snatched the carrot from her hand. "This is awesome!"

Jack gently stroked Beauty between her eyes. "Wouldn't it be cool to own a horse farm like this one?" he asked. "You could hang out with horses for, like, your job." His blue eyes shone as he spoke.

Hmm. Now, *this* was progress, Stephanie thought. Not only was she talking to Jack, he was telling her his dream of owning a farm! That had to mean something, right?

"I would love to spend more time talking

horses with you," Stephanie said as casually as possible. "I mean, I feel like I could learn so much from you."

Jack beamed. "Hey, why don't you sign up to volunteer here? Mr. Montgomery is always looking for new people. We can muck out the stalls together."

Stephanie wrinkled up her nose. Mucking out didn't sound very appealing. Also it wasn't exactly the kind of quality time with Jack that she had in mind.

Still, he was sort of saying he'd like to see her again. "I'll, uh, h-have to think about it," Stephanie stammered. "I have so many after-school activities."

Jack shrugged. "Whatever." He gave Beauty another pat on the head. "I've got some more straw to spread." He turned away from Stephanie and got to work. "See you later."

Ouch. Stephanie stood there, totally bummed out. *Way to go, Steph,* she thought. *You just blew your big opportunity.* The writers at *Teen Trends* could write an article about *her:* "How to Completely Blow It With the Perfect Guy."

Still—did she have to work at the stable to

get Jack to ask her to the dance? There had to be an easier way.

Maybe she could ask to borrow his history notes, or slip into the chair next to his at the next school assembly, or—

"Hey, Jack, want to finish my chores for me while I go for a nice, long ride?" a girl—who happened to have the shiniest brown hair Stephanie had ever seen—called out.

Jack stood up. "I did your chores yesterday. In fact, maybe I should let you finish mine for me today."

The girl laughed. "Not on your life!"

Stephanie didn't move. Whoa! Who was this girl? Stephanie had never seen her around school, but she did seem to know Jack pretty well.

Maybe too well.

"Stephanie, this is Theresa," Jack said.

"Nice to meet you, Theresa." Stephanie gave the girl a friendly smile.

Hold on, Stephanie told herself. *This girl is probably a volunteer at the stable.*

Yes. Theresa and Jack were probably just friends. Nothing more.

"Hi, Stephanie," Theresa said. She walked around to where Jack was standing. "Don't let Jack try to convince you that cleaning a stall is fun—he tried that on me once."

Jack slung an arm around Theresa's shoulders. "Hey, I needed a little help!" He laughed.

Stephanie laughed, too. But inside, she was full of doubt.

"Well, I've got to go find my sister," Stephanie said, excusing herself. "See you guys around."

Stephanie turned and moved toward the other end of the barn.

Jack still had an arm around that girl! Was she his girlfriend?

She couldn't be! Darcy and Allie had told Stephanie that Jack was available!

Maybe Jack and Theresa were just starting to get to know each other, Stephanie thought. Maybe they were *on the way* to becoming boyfriend and girlfriend.

I'll have Darcy and Allie ask around some more, Stephanie decided. *And I'll see if Michelle can get to the bottom of the story, too.*

Until then, there was only one answer. If she wanted Jack to ask her to the dance, she had to take action. Otherwise, Theresa was going to go out with Jack before she did.

Stephanie wasn't nuts about horses, but what choice did she have?

That's it, Stephanie decided. *I'm volunteering at this place.*

Goodbye, hanging out at the mall; hello, straw.

Chapter 5

I want ice cream!" Nicky yelled that evening. "I hate meat loaf!"

Michelle giggled. Preparing dinner in her house was always noisy. Everybody participated, and everybody had something to say. Usually, the twins' opinions were the loudest!

"Me, too!" Alex, Nicky's twin brother, shouted, quick to agree with Nicky. "Cookies 'N' Cream!"

Uncle Jesse picked up Nicky and swung him up and onto his shoulders. "Last time we had meat loaf, both of you guys had seconds. Am I right, or am I right?"

"And we're having ice cream for *dessert*," Michelle assured the twins.

"All right!" Alex punched his fist in the air and jumped up and down with excitement.

Michelle turned back to the head of iceburg lettuce she was tearing into bite-size pieces. She had spent the last hour trying to figure out a way to put her idea to save Chestnut into action. Maybe Nicky and Alex could provide the perfect lead-in.

"Hey, Nicky, what's your favorite kind of animal?" Michelle asked even though she already knew the answer.

"Horses!" Nicky answered. He dropped to the kitchen floor and began to neigh.

"Yeah, horses!" Alex agreed.

As the twins launched into a noisy game of "horsey," Michelle slid her cutting board full of lettuce toward her dad. He was chopping onions on the other end of the long counter.

"Speaking of horses, I have a brilliant idea, Dad," Michelle said.

"What is it, honey?" Danny set down his knife and turned his full attention to his daughter.

How to Hide a Horse

"Well, I heard a story on the radio about how people who have pets live to be older than people without pets."

Danny grinned. "I've heard the same thing. Pets relieve stress and give us humans the kind of unconditional love that makes us want to live as long as possible." He reached out and patted Michelle on the shoulder. "It's lucky for us that we have Comet, huh?"

Michelle nodded. "Yeah, but don't you think that with so many of us living in the house we need more than one pet?"

Danny raised his eyebrows. "Uh, Michelle, is this where the horse part comes in?"

"For the sake of family health, I think we should buy a horse," Michelle blurted out. She paused for a moment. "His name is Chestnut, and he's really small. He wouldn't be any trouble—I promise."

Danny smiled. He scooped up some tiny pieces of onion and tossed them into the big salad bowl. "It's a wonderful thought, Michelle—"

"I already thought everything through," Michelle interrupted. "He can stay in the backyard. And I know Nicky and Alex will help me take care of him. They love horses!"

"As I said, it's a nice idea—" Danny started to say.

"But?" Michelle asked. She could tell there was a *but* at the end of her dad's sentence.

"*But* a horse needs a lot of special attention. Our backyard isn't big enough for that kind of animal." Danny squeezed her shoulders. "Where would he run? And where would he go when it rains?"

Michelle's heart sank. She had known, deep down, that her father wasn't going to agree to buy Chestnut from Mr. Montgomery. She had allowed herself to hold out just a teeny bit of hope.

"Never mind, Dad," she whispered. "I know you're right."

Michelle stared at the remainder of the lettuce and allowed her thoughts to wander. So much for Plan A to save Chestnut from having to work in New York City. Michelle was going to have to do some major thinking—fast. She had less than three days to come up with a Plan B.

Suddenly, D.J. nudged her in the side. "If you're not going to finish tearing the lettuce, let me take over."

Michelle shrugged. "Fine by me."

She moved away from the counter and bumped right into Stephanie.

"Michelle! My sweet, dear little sister—" Stephanie threw an arm around Michelle's shoulders as she steered her toward the one empty corner of the large kitchen.

"Uh-oh," Michelle interrupted her sister. "You're calling me 'sweet' and 'dear.' Something is definitely up."

"I need a favor," Stephanie admitted.

"From me? What is it?" Michelle asked.

"I saw Jack talking to a girl at the stable today," Stephanie told her. "I need you to find out whether or not she's his girlfriend."

Wow! This was a switch. Usually, Michelle was the one asking *Stephanie* for a favor. And this favor wasn't taking her sister's turn washing the dishes. This favor was boy related! It was so grown-up.

"Is that all?" Michelle asked. "No problem."

"But, listen. You can't be obvious about it,"

Stephanie cautioned. "Try to find out without actually coming out and asking him."

"Leave everything to me," Michelle told her.

"And I need to know soon," Stephanie said. "It's very, very important."

"Jack. Girlfriend," Michelle said. "Got it."

"Thanks!" Stephanie spun away from Michelle and went back to setting the table.

Now that that was settled, Michelle could go back to thinking about her big problem, Chestnut.

Plan B. Plan B. I need a Plan B. Michelle squeezed her eyes shut and tried to drown out the noise of her family. Who could think with all of these people around? After dinner Michelle would have to lock herself in her room and wait for an idea to find its way into her brain.

"Michelle? Earth to Michelle Tanner." Aunt Becky's voice broke into Michelle's thoughts.

"Yes, Aunt Becky?" Michelle returned to her place at the kitchen counter and picked up a carrot. She began peeling like crazy. The faster everything was done, the faster she could plan exactly how she was going to save Chestnut.

Aunt Becky laughed. "I was just telling everyone that your dad and I interviewed Samantha Gilmore on the show this morning. She's the head zookeeper at the San Francisco Zoo, and she's offered to take all of us on a private tour of the new petting zoo. I wanted to know if you'd like to come along."

Aunt Becky and Michelle's dad were co-hosts of a local morning talk show *Wake Up, San Francisco*. They interviewed cool people all the time.

"Petting zoo?" Michelle brightened. "That sounds pretty fun."

"We're going to see a goat!" Alex yelled.

"And a rabbit!" Nicky exclaimed.

"And an ostrich and a penguin—" Alex continued.

"I don't think there are going to be any penguins at the petting zoo, bud," Uncle Jesse said with a laugh. "And we probably won't see any polar bears, either."

"Horses!" Nicky shouted.

Horses? Wait a minute. Michelle could feel

it. She was about to have a brilliant, amazing idea. . . .

A new petting zoo needed cute little foals! Foals like Chestnut! Michelle thrust her carrot into her Aunt Becky's hands and sprinted out of the kitchen.

She needed to call Annie at the stable right away. Plan B was a go. Michelle was going to save Chestnut, after all!

STEPHANIE

Chapter
6

Stephanie studied herself in the dusty mirror that hung on the back of the door in Sunset Farm's small bathroom.

She surveyed the outfit she had changed into for her first day as a stable volunteer.

Over all, she was happy with the effect of her choices—faded blue jeans, a red-and-white-checked flannel shirt, and a pair of red cowboy boots Stephanie had bought at a clearance sale. She had known there would be a time when she needed the boots, and now was the time. Jack would have to be impressed with her western gear.

"You love working with the horses," Stephanie coached her reflection. "You're a supremo horsewoman."

She strode out of the bathroom feeling confident. How bad could this volunteering stuff be? Mr. Montgomery would probably just ask her to file a bunch of papers in his office.

Then, during a break, she could approach Jack and start another conversation. Even better, maybe *he* would start talking to *her*.

"Hi, Stephanie!" Mr. Montgomery boomed, walking out of the office. Stephanie gazed at the tall, broad-shouldered man. He ran a hand through his short, wavy, sandy-brown hair. "You're just in time for a very important job."

"I'm ready, willing, and able," Stephanie announced.

She glanced around the stable. Good. She didn't see Theresa anywhere. Maybe today Stephanie would have Jack's undivided attention. *Once he shows up, that is,* she added to herself.

"Here's a pitchfork," Mr. Montgomery said, handing Stephanie the same one Jack had been using the day before. "And there is Amazon's stall." He pointed across the barn. "Just spread around some fresh straw."

Stephanie wrinkled her nose.

Well, here goes nothing, she thought. Gripping the pitchfork with both hands, Stephanie headed toward Amazon's stall. *This will all be worth it,* she thought. *As soon as Jack asks me to the dance!*

Forty-five minutes later Stephanie felt as if her back were on fire. Muscles she had never known she had were screaming in pain. As for the way she *smelled*—she didn't even want to think about that.

"All this work for nothing," Stephanie muttered to herself. She hadn't caught even a glimpse of Jack since she rushed to Sunset Farm after school.

Mr. Montgomery appeared outside Buttercup's stall, where Stephanie was currently "mucking out."

"How's it going, Steph?" he asked. "Are you enjoying your first day as a volunteer?"

Stephanie resisted the urge to groan. "I'm having a terrific time, Mr. Montgomery."

Now that she was standing still, Stephanie became very aware that her awesome red cowboy boots were at least one size too small. She could feel blisters forming on each and every one of her ten toes.

"Keep up the good work," Mr. Montgomery told her. "You're going to be a real asset around here."

Stephanie sighed as he turned and headed back toward his office. She didn't have to look in a mirror to know that ribbons of sweat were running down her face. She probably looked like a wreck.

At this point all she could hope was that Jack *didn't* show up. If he saw her now, the guy would probably run away in fright.

"Hey, Stephanie."

Yikes! Jack's voice sent a jolt up Stephanie's spine.

For a split second Stephanie hoped that the floor of the stable would open up and swallow her whole. When that didn't happen, she reached up to tuck several loose strands of hair behind her ears. Then she flashed Jack a friendly smile. "Hi, Jack."

"Hey. I'm psyched you decided to make time for the farm." His voice was warm and definitely friendly.

"Yeah, I'm having a blast." *Aside from the fact that my hair is a frizz ball and I'm aching all over,* she added to herself.

Jack's gaze moved from the pitchfork to Stephanie's sweaty face. "Just a wild guess, Steph, but is this your first time spreading straw in a stable?"

Terrific. She wasn't only a mess, she obviously had no idea what she was doing! Way to impress the horse guy, she thought.

Then again, Jack had called her "Steph" twice now. According to the *Teen Trends* article, a guy using your nickname was a positive sign for romance. All hope was not lost.

"Actually, I think I've become something of a straw expert during the last hour." Stephanie laughed.

Jack laughed, too. "Don't worry. It gets easier."

All right! Stephanie and Jack were having a normal conversation—and she didn't even feel shy.

"Maybe you could teach me some horse . . . stuff . . . sometime," Stephanie suggested.

Jack nodded. "I'd love to."

There was a moment of awkward silence during which Stephanie stared at the tips of her red cowboy boots. This was the hard part. How could she steer the conversation in the direction of the dance?

"So, um, how much volunteering did you sign up for?" Jack asked.

Stephanie gulped. This fell under the category of a trick question. Ninety percent of her wanted to tell Jack that she would be at the stable every afternoon after school. Ten percent of her—a *strong* ten percent—longed to tell Jack that the only reason she was at the stable was to get to know him. Or something.

"I'm, uh, I'm not sure yet," Stephanie finally answered. "Mr. Montgomery and I haven't worked out the details."

Stephanie hated fibbing. She also hated the fact that she was conversing with the cutest boy at John Muir Middle School with enough sweat to fill San Francisco Bay running down her face. She fiddled with a rope that was hanging from the ceiling of Buttercup's stall, hoping to calm her nerves.

"I'm here almost every day," Jack said. "Maybe we could make the trip from school together sometimes."

Stephanie smiled. She and Jack sharing public transportation was good. Very good.

"Yeah! That would be awesome." Stephanie felt something nagging at her. An idea.

This was her opportunity, she thought. She and Jack were having a great conversation, and he seemed to like her. Why not ask him to the dance herself?

Yes, she decided. She'd do it.

"Um, Jack," she started. "There's something I was wondering. . . ."

She put a little more of her weight on the rope, attempting a casual Julia Roberts–style lean against the stall wall.

"Wait, Stephanie, don't—" Jack started.

Oh, no! The thick rope in Stephanie's hand suddenly gave way. "Aaaah!" she yelped.

A mountain of hay fell from the ceiling— onto Jack's and Stephanie's heads!

She snapped her gaze upward—oops. The

rope was attached to the trapdoor of a hayloft. Oh, no. *Why* hadn't she realized that?

Stephanie sneezed, sending small bits of prickly hay flying in every direction. "Sorry, Jack."

Ugh! Stephanie wanted to crawl into the hay and never come out. If this was how she planned on getting Jack to take her to the dance, she'd better start planning on going solo.

MICHELLE

Chapter
7

It will be weird having a lesson without you," Mandy told Michelle after school.

"Saving Chestnut is more important than trying to convince Sabrina to let me do a jump," Michelle pointed out. "If we don't do something, Chestnut is going to spend the rest of her life breathing smoggy air and eating polluted grass."

Michelle was skipping her riding lesson to go with Aunt Becky, Uncle Jesse, and the twins to the petting zoo. It was time to put Plan B into action.

"Okay," Cassie said. "But we still don't understand exactly what your plan is."

"Trust me," Michelle said confidently. "After today, we're not going to have to worry about Chestnut anymore."

"Why is it such a secret?" Mandy groaned. "Can't you at least give us a hint?"

"I don't want to jinx it," Michelle explained, her eyes twinkling. "But I promise I'll tell you everything—*after* I'm sure Chestnut will be safe!"

"There's Samantha," Aunt Becky announced. "Let the petting zoo tour begin!"

Michelle followed Aunt Becky's gaze. A very pretty young woman stood next to a peanut vendor near the entrance of the San Francisco Zoo. She was smiling and waving at everyone.

Samantha looks nice, Michelle decided. Good. She wanted Chestnut to be with nice people only.

"Hi, everyone!" Samantha greeted them. "I'm glad you could make it."

As Aunt Becky introduced everyone to the head zookeeper, Michelle continued to study Samantha. She had bright red hair and twinkling blue eyes. Samantha Gilmore looked just like the kind of woman who would want to save a sweet, gentle foal from a horrible life.

The group followed Samantha to a special entrance. WELCOME TO THE NEW ZOO, a sign read.

"Before we start looking around, let me tell you a little about the petting zoo," Samantha said. "Our goal is to allow zoo visitors to interact with some of their favorite animals."

"Cool!" Nicky yelled.

"Follow me," Samantha said. "I'll give you a quick tour, and then we can spend more time with the animals you like best."

The group followed Samantha past several geese, a donkey, and two ostriches. Michelle studied the animals carefully as she walked past them. They all seemed calm and happy. The petting zoo wasn't big, but there were lots of trees, and all the animals had plenty of room to roam around.

It seemed like it would be a really good place for Chestnut.

"Do you have all the animals for the petting zoo yet?" Michelle asked when the group stopped.

Samantha shook her head. "Nope. We're

still in the process of acquiring animals." She glanced at Nicky and Alex. "But we've got enough to keep two boys busy for quite some time!"

Perfect. If the zoo was still adopting animals, maybe they'd want Chestnut!

Samantha led the group to an ultra-big fenced-in enclosure. The large space was grassy with a big pond in the middle. Several ducks swam in the water. Others waddled around, pecking at pieces of bread.

Samantha pointed across the wide path that divided the petting zoo. "Over there we have a family of goats."

"Hello, goats," Michelle greeted two baby goats who were grazing in the small pasture.

This petting zoo sure was nice, Michelle thought. Chestnut would have lots of friends here. She walked a few feet farther and saw two—what were those things? Michelle leaned close and read a small typed label. "Hello, llamas!" she said. Wow. She had never seen a llama before.

Samantha started to walk again, and the group followed. Nicky and Alex were tugging on Samantha's sleeves as they shouted out questions. Michelle continued to study the petting zoo.

There was a flock of sheep. Over farther she saw several rabbit hutches. There was even a bunch of turtles. As far as she could tell, there was no horse. Plan B was looking better than ever.

"Want to pet a real live peacock, Michelle?" Uncle Jesse asked, breaking into Michelle's thoughts.

Michelle nodded. "In a minute." She had a lot more important things on her mind—like how to get Samantha Gilmore alone so that she could ask her about Chestnut.

"Um, Samantha, can I ask you a question about the llamas?" Michelle asked.

"Of course." Samantha followed her to the llamas. "What is it you want to know, Michelle?"

"Actually, I was wondering whether or not . . . oomph." Michelle doubled over as Alex suddenly lunged at her.

"I'm scared!" he shouted. "The peacock snapped at me!"

Samantha laughed. "He's just guarding his territory, sweetie. Don't worry. He's harmless."

Nicky tugged on Samantha's hand. "Can we see the bunnies now?"

Samantha smiled an apology. "I guess your question will have to wait, Michelle. These cousins of yours are quite a handful."

"Tell me about it," Michelle said grumpily. She loved the twins more than anything, but sometimes their timing was terrible.

At the rabbit hutches Michelle cradled a baby bunny. Usually, holding such a tiny ball of fluff would be heaven. Now all Michelle could think about was convincing Samantha to buy Chestnut for the petting zoo.

She placed the bunny carefully into its hutch. Several feet away, Aunt Becky and Uncle Jesse were talking with Samantha.

Michelle strode quickly over to them. "Alex and Nicky want to show you two something," she told her aunt and uncle. "I'll keep Samantha company."

Alex and *Nicky* were the magic words. Immediately Becky and Jesse headed toward their sons, just as Michelle knew they would.

This was it. The moment of truth.

"I noticed that the petting zoo doesn't have any horses," Michelle said.

Samantha nodded. "Not yet. But we're planning to get at least one. I just haven't found the right foal yet."

Michelle grinned. She felt like jumping into the zookeeper's arms and hugging her tight. "If you're looking for a foal, I know the perfect horse for you!"

"Really? What horse is that?" Samantha asked.

"His name is Chestnut. He's small and gentle, and he has the prettiest brown eyes I've ever seen, and—"

"Whoa," Samantha interrupted, laughing. "Slow down a second."

Michelle took a deep breath. "Sorry—I'm just so excited." She paused again. "I know that this horse really, really needs a good home. He lives at Sunset Farm right now, but his owners need to sell him."

Samantha nodded. "I know Sunset Farm. Tom Montgomery owns it, doesn't he?"

"Right!" Michelle told her. "Mr. Montgomery is a nice man, but he's planning to sell Chestnut to some people in New York City. And that's no place for a little horse."

Samantha nodded. "Well, we certainly need to buy a foal." She thought for a moment. "I'll tell you what, Michelle. Tomorrow morning I'll talk to some people here at the zoo and give Tom a call. If we can work out the details, Chestnut can have a brand-new home right here."

Yes! Michelle felt like dancing. Plan B had worked. Chestnut was going to have a good home—one where Michelle could visit him anytime she wanted.

STEPHANIE

Chapter 8

Charlie finally asked me to the dance!" Allie repeated for the fifth time in the past fifteen minutes.

Stephanie smiled at her friend.

"I can't believe it. He just came right out and asked me," Allie continued.

"There's nothing that surprising about it," Mrs. Taylor said from the driver's seat of the Taylors' minivan. "It seems to me that the boy just came to his senses."

Mrs. Taylor was dropping Stephanie off at Sunset Farm for volunteer duty. Then she was taking Darcy and Allie to the mall. While

Stephanie was working in the barn, her best friends planned to shop for dresses for the dance. What she wouldn't give to trade places with them.

"Exactly," Darcy agreed with Mrs. Taylor. "I knew Charlie would get smart and see you as the cool chick you are."

Stephanie sank farther down into the vinyl seats in the back of the minivan. Now that Charlie Rubin had come through with an invitation to the John Muir Middle School dance, both Allie and Darcy had dates.

The pressure was on. Stephanie *really* had to get a date. She didn't think she would feel comfortable being a fifth wheel at the dance.

Mrs. Taylor flipped on her blinker and turned onto the road that led to Sunset Farm. Allie peered at Stephanie from the front seat. "How's it going with Jack?"

Stephanie groaned. "Aside from the fact that I dumped a mountain of straw on him yesterday? Fine."

Darcy giggled. "Steph, he's a horse guy. Jack probably sleeps on a straw mattress."

"Yeah. It's really not a big deal, Stephanie," Allie pointed out.

"I still think I have to do something special to impress him today," Stephanie insisted.

"Maybe you shouldn't do anything until we find out more about this mystery girl," Allie suggested. "If she's his girlfriend, all your plotting could be for nothing."

"Don't even *say* it!" Stephanie said. "I can't consider the idea that I don't have a chance."

"Well, I hope things work out for you, Stephanie," Mrs. Taylor said as she stopped the car in front of the entrance of Sunset Farm. "But my advice is just be yourself. That's always the best route to take."

"Thanks." Stephanie hopped out of the car. She waved good-bye to her friends and Mrs. Taylor, then headed toward the barn.

"Ready to saddle up some horses?" Joe, the stable hand, asked as soon as Stephanie entered the barn.

"Um—sure—I guess." Stephanie bit her lip. Not that she knew anything about saddling a horse.

Prepare to make a fool of yourself. Day Two, she thought.

Joe dumped a large saddle into Stephanie's outstretched arms.

Oomph. It was *heavy*—and full of lots of straps and buckles.

Stephanie stared at the saddle in her hands. What now?

"Need some help with that saddle, cowgirl?"

Stephanie turned around. Jack! She grinned at him broadly. "Actually, yes. Totally. I need all the help I can get here."

Hmmm, Stephanie thought. Jack had approached *her* and offered to help. A good omen. She followed him to Buttercup's stall, her heart beating crazily inside her chest.

"Putting a saddle on a horse is easy," Jack told her as he took the saddle from her arms. "It's all about using your common sense."

"Got it. Common sense." Stephanie watched Jack gently place the saddle onto Buttercup's long back.

He lifted a dangling beltlike piece of leather and placed it in Stephanie's hands. "Now buckle this, over there."

Stephanie followed his instructions. Luckily, Buttercup remained calm. She seemed happy to have Stephanie and Jack attaching the saddle to her back. Stephanie began to relax. That was easy!

"I think I'm getting this," she said excitedly.

Jack grinned. "Now you wait for the horse to exhale. That's it. Now tighten the girth around his belly . . . right! Now Buttercup is ready for her lesson."

Stephanie gestured to the saddled horse. "Ta-da!"

"Great job, Steph. I think you're ready to do the next saddle all on your own."

"Cool!" This chore was turning out better than Stephanie ever could have hoped. Especially since she and Jack seemed to be hitting it off.

Ask me to the dance. Ask me to the dance. Stephanie hoped her telepathic message was getting through to Jack loud and clear.

"Stephanie? Did you hear me?"

She blinked. Oops. "I was—uh—going over your directions in my head," Stephanie said, recovering quickly. "I'm ready for the next saddle."

They walked the few steps to Amazon's stall. "Try it on your own," Jack instructed. "I'll be right here, inspecting the rest of the stall. Jack handed Stephanie another saddle. "Go for it."

Stephanie slipped the saddle onto Amazon's back. Step one. Check. She fastened the girth under the horse's body. Step two. Check. Hey, this really was pretty easy. Jack had been right. "Attach this, buckle that," Stephanie whispered to herself.

A loud giggle across the room caught Stephanie's attention, breaking her concentration. She glanced up from her task and gazed in the direction of the sound. It was Theresa, the mystery girl. She was in the middle of a major laugh fest with one of the other stable volunteers—a boy.

The two looked friendly. Very friendly. In fact, they looked *so* friendly that Stephanie thought maybe they could be a couple.

Could this day get any better? Stephanie wondered. Yes, it could.

I'm going to try again. I'm going to ask Jack to the dance, she decided. *Right now.*

She had mastered saddling a horse today. Why not master the art of asking a guy out? If Darcy could do it, so could Stephanie.

"Jack, there's something I want to ask you," Stephanie began. She could feel her cheeks burning.

"Sure, Steph." Jack turned toward her. They were just inches apart from each other.

"I, uh . . ." She paused.

"Oh, good, Amazon is ready to ride," Sabrina, Michelle's riding instructor, said, walking up to them. "If you two don't mind, I'll go ahead and lead him outside." She grabbed Amazon's reins and started off with him.

"I wanted to ask you if—" Stephanie stopped midsentence. Jack's face had totally changed.

"What the—" Jack shouted.

Oh, no. Somehow, Amazon was *pulling* Jack behind him. How was that possible?

Stephanie quickly glanced at Amazon's saddle. A rope with a loop had become tangled around Amazon's saddle and was now wrapped around Jack's leg.

"Stop!" Jack shouted. The rope pulled tight.

Jack started hopping behind Amazon to keep from falling over.

His shouting seemed to startle Amazon. The horse picked up speed and broke away from Sabrina. He ran across the open floor of the barn and headed into the corral.

"Aaah!" Jack yelped. He lost his balance and fell to the ground, a cloud of dust rising around him.

Amazon continued to run, dragging Jack behind him. Everyone outside watched, their mouths hanging open.

"Oh, no!" Stephanie gasped.

As Sabrina ran toward Jack, Stephanie raced toward the other side of the stable. Thanks to her, Jack was in danger! He needed help!

She pounded on Mr. Montgomery's office door. The least she could do was save Jack's life—or get someone who could!

One thing was for sure, Stephanie thought. This was no way to get a boyfriend!

MICHELLE

Chapter 9

Come on, Michelle!" Cassie begged. "Please tell us about Plan B!"

Michelle leaned casually against the fence that surrounded the corral.

"We are dying to know how you saved Chestnut!" Mandy agreed. "You have to tell us!"

Michelle glanced from one friend to the other. Both girls had been asking questions about her mysterious absence the day before, but Michelle kept her lips sealed.

She wanted to tell Mandy and Cassie about the petting zoo as much as they wanted to know about it. She didn't want to spill the beans until everything was settled.

"Hey, there's Annie in the far corral," Michelle announced. "As soon as I talk to her, I can tell you everything."

The girls descended upon Annie, who was busy saddling up her own horse, Road Runner. When she saw her new friends, Annie smiled.

Michelle couldn't wait another second to get the good news. "What did your dad say when Samantha Gilmore called?" she asked excitedly.

Annie frowned. "Huh? Who is Samantha Gilmore?"

Uh-oh. This was not a good sign.

"Samantha Gilmore is the lady from the petting zoo!" Michelle wailed. "She *promised* she would call to speak to your dad about the zoo adopting Chestnut."

"Wow!" Cassie said.

"What a great idea!" Mandy chimed in.

Annie shook her head sadly. "A great idea that's going nowhere. No one called to ask anything about Chestnut."

"I don't understand." Michelle had been so sure that Chestnut's problems were solved. Now she didn't know *what* to think.

"Here's the worst part," Annie said. "The new owner is planning to pick up Clancy and Chestnut tomorrow!" Tears shone in her eyes. "We're running out of time!"

"Poor Chestnut. Instead of playing with little kids, he's going to be hauling tourists around the middle of New York City." Cassie sighed. "But I guess there's nothing we can do now."

"Don't say that," Michelle told her. "I just have to think of another plan."

"Hey, what's going on?" Mandy asked. "Everyone's yelling!"

The girls raced toward the scene. Michelle stared as Amazon dragged Jack around the corral. It looked as if Jack's foot was caught in a rope attached to Amazon's saddle. Everybody was running after Amazon, trying to free Jack.

Michelle had no idea what had happened, but Jack's timing was perfect!

"Quick!" Michelle called to her friends. "I've got an idea!"

Mandy, Cassie, and Annie followed Michelle into the barn. Michelle stopped in front of Chestnut's stall. The little foal whinnied happily as soon as he saw her.

"Don't worry, Chestnut. We'll take care of you." She reached into the stall and softly petted Chestnut's shiny brown mane.

"What are you doing, Michelle?" Annie asked.

Michelle gazed ahead. "We have to hide Chestnut so that he won't get shipped to New York before Samantha calls."

"Great idea, but there's one problem," Cassie pointed out. "How do you hide a horse?"

"Yeah, and *where* do we hide him?" Mandy asked Annie.

Annie thought for a moment. "I know a place, but I'm not so sure this is a good idea."

"Come on," Cassie urged. "Chestnut's happiness is the most important thing here."

Annie bit her lip.

"If we don't do *something*, he's going to be shipped off to New York City tomorrow," Michelle reminded Annie.

"All right. Let's do it!" Annie smiled. "There's an abandoned barn on the far side of the pasture. We can slip Chestnut out the side door to get there."

"Great. Let's hurry," Michelle whispered.

Everyone was still focused on Jack, who was tangled up in Amazon's long reins. Who knew how long it would take them to notice what the girls were doing? Michelle knew there wasn't a second to spare.

Annie bridled Chestnut and led him out of the stall. Mandy grabbed a bucket of oats. Cassie picked up a bale of hay.

"Let's do this right," Michelle said. " After all, Chestnut is counting on us!"

Annie headed for the side door. Cassie, Mandy, and Michelle followed quickly, trying not to make too much noise on the creaky wooden floor.

"Open the door, Michelle!" Annie instructed.

Michelle sidled around her friends and pushed open the door of the barn. She held the door as the group filed through. As soon as Michelle shut the door behind them, they would be home free.

"Hey, where are you girls heading?" Joe, the stable hand, called across the barn.

Michelle gulped. She didn't think anyone had seen Chestnut leave the barn, but she didn't want to blow the secret. What should she say?

Suddenly Annie's head popped back into the barn. "I'm going to show Mandy, Cassie, and Michelle the tree house my dad built for me when I was little," she called.

Joe nodded. "Oh, okay. Have fun." He turned and left the barn.

"Whew. That was a close one!" Michelle said when everyone was outside. "Annie, you really saved the day."

"This way!" Annie exclaimed. "The barn is on the other side of the farm."

Michelle picked up her pace. In near silence the girls jogged all the way across the farm. Chestnut trotted alongside, almost as if he knew that a plan was in action.

"Are we getting close?" Mandy panted after several minutes.

"It's not far now," Annie answered her.

"I think I see the barn," Cassie exclaimed.

"Is that it?" She pointed to a small structure in the distance.

"Yep. That's it," Annie confirmed.

Michelle turned back and looked at the main barn. It seemed so far away. "You'll be safe soon, Chestnut."

Chestnut neighed and tossed his head from side to side.

Michelle laughed. "I love you, too," she told the little foal. Now she was more sure than ever that she was doing the right thing. Chestnut had practically told her so with his nickering!

Michelle clasped the colt's mane and sprinted the rest of the way toward the small barn. The wind blew back her hair and filled her lungs. Beside her, Chestnut trotted on his small, delicate legs.

In moments they had reached the barn. "Stop, Chestnut," Michelle called.

The horse slowed to a walk, then halted in front of the barn door. "Good boy," Michelle praised him.

The barn door squeaked loudly when Michelle slid it open. Inside, the building's structure appeared solid. Light shone through several holes in the ceiling, but the floor was firm.

Annie entered the barn. Mandy and Cassie were close behind. "Nobody ever comes to this barn anymore," Annie informed them. "No one will look for Chestnut here."

"You're amazing," Michelle told Annie. "If we manage to save Chestnut, he has you to thank."

"And you," Annie said. "I would never have thought of this on my own."

Annie walked Chestnut over to an ancient, roomy stall. Mandy and Cassie arranged the oats and the hay. At last everything seemed to be in order.

Michelle stood close to Chestnut's side. "You're safe—for now," she whispered to the foal. "But I hope Samantha Gilmore calls soon. We can't hide you forever!"

STEPHANIE

Chapter
10

Stephanie walked out of John Muir Middle School with Darcy and Allie the next day. She replayed the scene at the stable the day before over and over in her mind.

Ugh! The whole thing was so mortifying.

If she hadn't promised Danny she would take Michelle to her riding lesson, Stephanie definitely wouldn't be showing her face at Sunset Farm that afternoon. Especially since Theresa comforted Jack after the disaster with Amazon.

Who is that girl? Stephanie wondered.

"You've been frowning all day, Steph," Darcy commented. "What's up?"

Stephanie groaned. "Trust me. You don't want to know."

"Trust *us*. We *do* want to know," Allie answered. "Spill it."

Stephanie sighed. "I made a complete fool of myself in front of Jack—again. He probably hates me."

"What happened?" Darcy demanded. "Did you accidentally dump hay all over him again?"

"The hay was nothing compared to what happened yesterday," Stephanie answered glumly. "I practically killed him!"

Allie patted Stephanie on the back. "It can't be that bad, Steph. I saw him in school today."

Stephanie sighed. She had seen Jack, too. He nodded at her in the hallway between classes but hadn't bothered to say hello. There was no doubt about it. She was a walking disaster—and Jack knew it!

"The more I try to impress Jack, the more I look like a complete and total loser," Stephanie wailed.

"If you don't tell us exactly what happened, how can we rate its awfulness on a scale of one to ten—and figure out whether you're overreacting or not?" Darcy pointed out.

"Fine. Here goes—" Stephanie began. "I accidentally tied Jack to a horse when I was saddling it."

Allie clapped a hand over her mouth. "Whoops!"

"As soon as the horse took off, he dragged Jack with him." She moaned. "For, like, five minutes there was *total* chaos—and it was all because of me."

"But Jack was all right, wasn't he?" Darcy asked.

"Well, luckily, he didn't break anything, but he did get plenty of bruises," Stephanie explained.

"I still think you're overreacting," Allie said. "I mean, it's not like you turned Jack into a rodeo act on *purpose*."

"There's more," Stephanie said.

"More?" Darcy squeaked. "Wow. Looks like we're going for a perfect ten on the embarrass-o-meter."

"That other girl, Theresa, was there. She

rushed to Jack's side as soon as Amazon stopped dragging him across the floor."

"Double ouch," Allie said.

"Tell me about it," Stephanie answered.

"Still, for all you know, she's just a friend," Darcy reminded Stephanie. "Just a friend helping another friend who became attached to a large, rampaging four-legged animal."

The girls crossed the street and approached Michelle's school. Stephanie could see her little sister sitting on the front steps, waiting to be picked up.

"Did you get any info on the mystery girl from Michelle?" Allie asked Stephanie.

"Not yet. With everything that's been going on, I hadn't asked her if she was able to find anything out."

"Why don't you ask her now?" Allie suggested. "If it's bad news, you can skip the farm and drown your sorrows in a pizza at Anthony's with us."

"Hey, Michelle!" Darcy called. "You're just the cowgirl we were looking for!"

Michelle hopped to her feet. "What? Why

were you looking for me? I didn't do anything. Really."

Stephanie laughed. Sometimes her little sister seemed totally unconnected to reality.
"Michelle, *what* are you talking about?"

"Uh, never mind." Michelle swung her back-
pack onto her shoulders. "Let's get to the stable!"

"Wait!" Stephanie told her. "I want to know
if you found out anything!"

For a moment Michelle stared at her sister.
"Found out? Found out about what?"

"You know," Darcy said. "The dirt on Jack
and the girl from the barn."

"Oh." Michelle was silent for a few seconds.
"Ummmm—well, I think you should give up.
That other girl is almost definitely going to the
dance with Jack."

Stephanie's heart sank. "She is?"

"What's her last name?" Allie asked.
"Where does she go to school?"

"Her last name?" Michelle echoed. "Oh,
um, I don't know . . . exactly, but I, ah, overheard her and one of the other girls talking,"
Michelle said quickly. "She was talking about,
um, Jack and a dance and—"

"Are you *positive* about this, Michelle?" Stephanie asked.

Michelle shrugged. "No. I guess I'm not *positive*. I mean, I could have heard wrong. Yeah, I mean, don't go by what I say."

Stephanie sighed. There seemed to be only one way to find out the true story. She would have to have a conversation with Theresa— and get to the bottom of this once and for all.

Chapter
11

"Samantha Gilmore *still* hasn't called your dad about Chestnut?" Michelle asked Annie later that afternoon.

Annie sighed. "Nope. So far, no phone call."

Michelle's stomach flipped over. Chestnut was safe for then—but the girls couldn't hide him forever. Besides, Chestnut's new owner was scheduled to pick him up that day.

Annie had covered Chestnut's absence that morning by volunteering to feed the foal herself. But sooner or later someone was going to notice that the horse was missing.

"In the meantime, we should probably head

over to the old barn," Cassie commented. "Chestnut must be lonely all by himself."

"No problem. I told Sabrina that we were going out for a little trail ride together before your lesson."

"Great. Let's go," Michelle agreed. "I can't wait to see him."

"We need oats. We need water and straw." Cassie ticked off the items on her fingers.

"And don't forget the carrots and sugar cubes," Mandy added. "Chestnut deserves some treats."

Annie giggled. "Pretty soon you guys are going to know as much about horses as I do!"

Annie had already saddled the girls' favorite horses—Clancy, Amazon, Beauty, and Road Runner. In moments they were all mounted on their horses and moving toward the old abandoned barn.

"We're taking the back trail," Annie called. "I don't want anyone to see where we're going."

The girls followed Annie on a trail that led around a large pasture. In a single-file line the girls veered off into the woods. Under the trees it was cool and dark and peaceful. Michelle let her thoughts wander.

After we see Chestnut, I'll call Samantha myself, Michelle decided. *I'm positive that once I talk to her, she'll call Mr. Montgomery and buy Chestnut for the zoo.*

Fifteen minutes later the group emerged from the woods, the barn directly in front of them.

"We'll go around back to tie up the horses so no one sees them," Annie instructed. "Better safe than sorry."

At the back of the barn the girls slid off their horses. They slipped their reins around an old wooden pole. Each girl grabbed the item she had brought for Chestnut and walked toward the barn.

"Hi, Chestnut," Michelle called out as she entered the barn. "Hi, boy."

"Do you want some oats, Chestnut?" Cassie asked. "Yum, yum!"

The girls crowded into Chestnut's stall. Cassie held the bucket out to the horse. Normally, Chestnut would stick his nose in the bucket and begin eating immediately.

But now, something was wrong. Chestnut barely sniffed the oats.

"Why isn't he eating?" Mandy asked.

"I don't know," Annie answered. "Here, Michelle. Try a sugar cube."

Michelle took one of the white squares and held it out to the horse. "Come on, Chestnut, have a taste."

The horse just turned his head away.

"What's wrong with him?" Mandy asked. "The other day, Chestnut was gobbling up sugar cubes."

Annie frowned as she studied Chestnut.

Michelle knelt at the little foal's side. "Do you feel sick, Chestnut? Do you want some water?"

Chestnut usually nickers and shakes his mane when I talk to him, Michelle thought. *Now he's just standing there*. A chill crawled down Michelle's spine. Something was terribly wrong.

Annie shook her head. "His eyes do look a little dull. But otherwise he seems okay," she reported.

"What should we do?" Mandy asked her friends anxiously.

Annie peered more closely into the foal's eyes. "For now, let's give him some fresh water and leave the food for him."

"Does he need a veterinarian?" Cassie asked. "Maybe we should tell your dad."

"No! We can't!" Michelle insisted. "Not yet."

"Chestnut is a little down, but I don't think he needs a doctor," Annie decided. "We'll come back and check on him later. If he still seems sick, we'll figure out what to do."

The girls were quiet as they mounted their horses and headed back to the main stable.

What if the foal really got sick? Michelle thought. It would be all her fault. She would never forgive herself if her attempt to save Chestnut did him more harm than good.

She had to call Samantha Gilmore at the zoo right away. It was the only way to make sure Chestnut would be safe—and not have to go to New York City.

Back at the stable, Sabrina was waiting for the girls. "Let's go, everybody!" she called as soon as she saw them. "We're not going to have much time if we don't get moving."

"I have to, uh, put a Band-Aid on one of my

blisters first," Michelle said, climbing off Clancy's back. "It'll just take a minute."

"I'll help you find one, Michelle," Annie offered quickly. She expertly jumped from her horse. "This way."

Michelle followed Annie into the stable. Her heart was pounding. "Where are we going?" Michelle asked quietly.

Annie motioned Michelle forward and opened the door to Mr. Montgomery's office. "My dad usually checks all the fences around this time. Let's use his office for a minute."

The girls slipped into Mr. Montgomery's office. Annie shut the door behind them. "What do we do now?" she asked.

Michelle flipped through the San Francisco phone book on Mr. Montgomery's desk. There it was. The number to the San Francisco Zoo. "We get Samantha Gilmore to come down here right away," Michelle told her. She punched in the number and crossed her fingers.

"It's ringing," Michelle reported to Annie. *Ring. Ring. Ring. Ring.*

At last a voice came on the line. But it wasn't a real human voice. It was a recording. "Thank you for calling the San Francisco Zoo. Office hours are from eight o'clock A.M. to four o'clock P.M. Please call back during office hours. Your call is important to us."

Michelle slammed down the phone.

"No answer?" Annie asked.

Michelle shook her head. "We missed office hours by"—she glanced at her watch—"fifteen minutes."

"Oh, no!" Annie exclaimed. "Chestnut's new owner could be here any minute now. We'll have to send him to New York City!"

"Don't say that," Michelle said. "We'll figure something out. I know we will." She headed for the office door. "But right now I had better get to my lesson, or Sabrina will know something's up."

Annie and Michelle slipped out of Mr. Montgomery's office as quietly as they had entered. Halfway across the large barn, Michelle stopped in her tracks. Mr. Montgomery was right in front of them. "Have you girls seen Chestnut?" he asked as soon as he saw them.

Michelle froze in her spot.

"Uh—why?" she asked.

Mr. Montgomery frowned. "His new owner is on the way over. I want Chestnut in his stall when he gets here."

Annie and Michelle exchanged worried glances. *Say something,* Michelle urged Annie in her mind. *Say anything.*

"I, uh, actually think I *did* see Ch–Chestnut," Annie stammered. "Yes. I saw him a little while ago. Someone must have let him into the lower pasture for exercise."

Mr. Montgomery snapped his fingers. "Of course. I didn't look there." He patted Annie on the head. "Thanks, honey. You're a lifesaver."

Once Mr. Montgomery was gone, Michelle and Annie stared at each other. "Good job, Annie," Michelle whispered. "That was a close call!"

"But it's no solution," Annie whispered back. "He'll find out soon that Chestnut *isn't* in the lower pasture."

Annie was right. They had bought some time—but only a little. The girls simply *had* to figure out a way to get the foal to the petting zoo. But how?

STEPHANIE

Chapter 12

Stephanie had mucked out four stalls. She had fed three horses. Her duties for the afternoon were officially completed. She couldn't put it off any longer. It was time to approach Theresa.

Stephanie strolled across the barn. Theresa was sitting on a stool, bent over a saddle in her lap. She seemed to be examining it for damage.

"Uh, hi, Theresa," Stephanie said.

Theresa smiled. "Hey, Stephanie, how's it going?"

"Great. Just great."

Yeah, *great*, Stephanie thought. Now what do I say?

"Do you like working around the barn?" Theresa asked.

Stephanie nodded. "Yeah, um, Jack has been a big help. And he's lots of fun."

Theresa nodded. "Jack loves to kid around." She laughed.

"Yeah? I mean, really?" Stephanie asked. She had to keep Theresa talking.

Again Theresa nodded. "Yeah. And not just at the stable. You should see him at a scary movie," she said. "He gets totally into it! The guy screams louder than anyone else in the theater when a monster pops out of a closet."

Stephanie gulped. "Do you two go to the movies together often?" she asked.

"No, not too much," Theresa answered.

Well, at least that was a good sign. Now to make the next question sound totally casual.

"Hey, there's a dance coming up at the middle school. Do you know if Jack is going?" Stephanie asked.

"Jack told me all about the dance. He's definitely going," Theresa told her. "He loves to dance."

Stephanie took a deep breath. Time for the most important question. "Do you know if he's . . . going with anybody special?"

Theresa wiggled her eyebrows. "Not yet, but I think he's planning to ask someone soon—if you know what I mean."

Stephanie felt her heart sink. She knew what Theresa meant. Theresa expected Jack to ask her to the dance.

Then again, Stephanie thought, it hadn't happened yet. Maybe she still had a chance.

"Cool," Stephanie responded in the most casual way possible. "Well, I guess I'd better get back to my chores. See you around."

"Later," Theresa answered.

Stephanie wandered across the barn, mulling over the conversation. Theresa seemed pretty sure of the fact that Jack was going to ask her to the dance.

It doesn't matter, Stephanie decided. *I'm not giving up. I'm here. I still have a huge crush on Jack. Why not make one last, big effort to impress him?*

But what could she do?

Stephanie stopped in front of the giant bulletin board that was hung next to Mr. Montgomery's office. She gazed blankly at the list of chores assigned to everyone that day.

That was it! Maybe Stephanie could do one of Jack's chores for him! That would be a nice gesture.

Stephanie scanned the list and found Jack's chores. Hmm. Next to most of them was a red check mark. Jack was done with those. A few of the tasks obviously hadn't been completed yet, though.

"Number Seven: Groom Southpaw," Stephanie read aloud. "Number Eight: Feed Lightning."

Groom? She could groom. Stephanie had seen some of the other volunteers brushing the horses. It looked simple enough. But the task took quite some time. She would be doing Jack a huge favor by taking on the duty herself.

Once I do this, Jack will know how sorry I am about yesterday, Stephanie decided. *It's the absolute perfect favor.*

She walked to Southpaw's row of stalls. She was a beautiful chestnut-colored mare. Brushing her long mane and shiny coat might actually be fun.

And I certainly know a thing or two about brushing hair, Stephanie thought, running her fingers through her own long, blond locks. *I'll be a natural at this.*

Grabbing a brush off a nail on the wall, Stephanie approached the door of Southpaw's stall. "Ready for a nice new hairdo?" she asked the horse. "I'm going to make you look really pretty—then you can tell Jack what an awesome girl I am."

She unlatched the door of the stall. But before Stephanie could enter the small space, the horse charged out.

"Whoa!" Stephanie jumped out of the way to keep from being trampled. "Stop! Stop!" she yelled after the horse.

The horse wasn't listening. She tore through the barn and exited through the open front door.

Oh, no! Now the horse was completely loose on the farm!

Stephanie sprinted after the mare, still gripping the brush. "Southpaw, whoa!" she shouted. *"Whoa!"*

Saying whoa always worked in western movies, but just then the phrase seemed totally useless. The mare galloped forward.

Joe, the stable hand, appeared at Stephanie's side. "That's not Southpaw!" he yelled. "That's Lightning!"

"The same Lightning that I've heard people talking about?" Stephanie asked. "The craziest horse in the stable?"

Joe nodded. "That horse is wild. We've got to rein her in!"

Stephanie groaned. She had meant to open Southpaw's stall but unlatched Lightning's instead. This was the worst mistake she had made at the stable yet!

In horror, Stephanie watched as Lightning raced toward the back of the barn and the corral, where Michelle, Mandy, and Cassie were in the middle of their riding lesson. The horse snorted and bucked and found the gate that had been left open.

"Lightning, no!" Stephanie yelled. But she

might as well have been talking to herself. The horse had a mind of her own.

In a flash, Lightning galloped into and across the large corral, continuing to buck and snort as she ran.

Joe sprinted toward the horse. Several other stable hands raced out of the barn, too. Each one climbed the corral fence in record speed. Michelle, Cassie, and Mandy had abandoned their horses and run out of the corral to safety.

The stable hands circled Lightning. One bravely darted forward and grabbed the out-of-control mare around the neck. After several agonizing minutes, the horse finally allowed the hand to slip a rope around her neck.

Mr. Montgomery was standing at the side of the corral. He ran his hands through his hair. Stephanie had never seen the owner of Sunset Farm look so upset.

"Jack!" Mr. Montgomery shouted. "Where's Jack?"

Jack emerged from inside the barn. He was holding a brush exactly like the one Stephanie had in her hand. Oh, no! Jack had probably been grooming the *right* horse at exactly the same time that Stephanie had let the *wrong* one out of her stall.

"I'm right here, Mr. Montgomery! What's going on?" Jack called.

"Jack, this is very serious," Mr. Montgomery scolded. "I asked you to take special care and be sure to latch the stall after you fed Lightning, didn't I?"

"But I—" Jack started to explain.

"Jack, you have to be more cautious. Lives could have been at stake here," Mr. Montgomery interrupted. "I don't want to see this kind of thing happen again."

"Of course, sir," Jack answered softly. "I'm sorry."

Stephanie was frozen to her spot. *I am the world's biggest loser,* she told herself. *I can't even brush a horse's mane without creating a scene. And now it's all my fault that Jack's in trouble!*

Finally the stable hands got Lightning under control.

I don't want to tell Jack the truth about who let Lightning out of her stall, Stephanie thought. But she had to. If she didn't, guilt would eat away at her insides for days.

Stephanie took a deep breath. She slowly approached Jack, who barely seemed to notice she was there. "Uh, hi."

He looked up. "Hey, Stephanie." He paused. "I guess you saw what happened, huh?"

A weak, nervous giggle escaped from Stephanie's lips. "Yeah, it was pretty crazy. I guess horses can be unpredictable."

Jack kicked a pebble with the toe of his boot and frowned. "I wish I knew how Lightning got out of that stall. I'm *positive* I latched that gate after I fed her."

This time Stephanie managed to hold in her nervous laughter. She didn't think Jack was going to find anything funny in what she was about to say. "Actually, I know how Lightning got out. . . ."

Jack raised his eyebrows. "You do? How?"

"I wanted to do you a favor," Stephanie explained, trying to sound upbeat. "I mean, I felt so horrible about what happened yesterday."

"Go on," Jack said, his voice a lot less friendly than it had been in the past. Somehow he seemed to sense where Stephanie was going with this.

"I looked at your list of tasks. Grooming Southpaw seemed like a good way to say I'm sorry about yesterday—but I accidentally went into Lightning's stall instead—"

"And she got out." Jack finished.

Stephanie nodded. "I'm really sorry, Jack. I'll go tell Mr. Montgomery right now that it was my fault."

Jack shook his head. "Please, don't. You've caused me enough trouble for one day."

"But—"

"Just stay away from me, Stephanie." Jack backed away from her. "You are totally bad news! I don't want you anywhere near me. Understand?"

Stephanie understood all right. She understood that as of that moment, her chances of getting Jack to take her to the dance were completely, absolutely shot.

Chapter
13

Lightning being loose in the corral was pretty scary, Michelle thought, but it was a really great distraction. Annie, Michelle, Cassie, and Mandy all glanced at one another, then slipped away to check on Chestnut.

Michelle and Annie slowed to a walk as they neared Chestnut's hiding place. Annie pulled a thick hardback book out from inside her denim jacket. She handed the book to Michelle.

"Diagnosing Horses," Michelle read. "What is this?"

"I took it from my dad's office while everyone was trying to round up Lightning," Annie explained. "It's a veterinary textbook he uses when he's trying to figure out what might be wrong with one of the horses."

"Do you think you'll be able to figure out what's wrong with Chestnut?" Michelle asked as they exited the woods.

Annie shrugged. "I'm sure going to try."

The girls walked into the barn and headed straight for Chestnut's stall. The foal didn't look any better than he had earlier. He barely blinked when he saw Annie and Michelle.

Instead, his head hung sadly.

"Chestnut hasn't touched the food we brought," Michelle said anxiously. "Not even the carrots."

Annie pulled up a dusty wood stool to the side of the stall and perched on top of it. She opened the big book across her lap and flipped through the pages.

"Tell me his symptoms," she instructed. "I'll try to match them up with one of the descriptions in here."

Michelle studied Chestnut for several moments. "He doesn't seem to have any energy," she announced.

"No energy," Annie noted. "What else?"

"Well, we also know that his appetite is gone." She peered into the fresh bucket of water they had left. "And he doesn't seem to be too thirsty, either."

"No energy. No appetite. Not thirsty." Annie skimmed through several pages. "So far, Chestnut's symptoms match every single thing that could be wrong with a horse."

"And his eyes are dull," Michelle added. "It's like he's not even looking at us."

"Hmm . . ." Annie kept reading, turning the pages in silence. "He could have a kind of flu that young horses often get." She paused. "Or it could be a cold."

"His coat doesn't look as brown and shiny as it usually does," Michelle commented. "Does that mean anything?"

"Coat not shiny." Annie flipped to the back of the book and scanned the index. "That particular symptom has, like, fifteen listings."

"Keep reading," Michelle urged. "Maybe there's one sickness that has *all* of Chestnut's symptoms."

Annie hunched over the book. As she studied the text, Michelle stroked Chestnut's side. "Try to eat something," she whispered to the foal. "You need to keep up your strength."

But Chestnut didn't respond to Michelle's soft encouragement. This was bad—really bad.

Finally Annie shook her head. "This book doesn't help at all."

"You have no idea what's wrong?" Michelle asked. "Not even a hint?"

"It could be *anything*," Annie said. "I just don't know."

"I'm going to try to call Samantha again," Michelle declared. "Maybe there's another number at the zoo where I can talk to a person—not a recording."

"Good idea," Annie agreed. "I'm going to stay here a little while and try to get Chestnut to eat something."

Michelle gave the foal one last kiss, then headed out of the barn. She was sure that once she told Samantha Gilmore that Chestnut was sick, the zookeeper would realize how important it was for Chestnut to get to her new home.

Michelle stood outside the barn for a moment, thinking about which route to take back to the main barn. The wooded path was the most hidden way. But it was also the longest. *Every minute counts*, Michelle reminded herself. She needed to get to a phone *right away*.

I'll cut through the upper pasture and hope that nobody wonders why I'm there. "Don't worry, Chestnut," she said aloud. "I'm not going to let you down."

Michelle sped up, turning her jog into a run. Out of the corner of her eye, in the field below her, Michelle suddenly saw a flash of blue denim. *What's that?*

She slowed down, then stopped. A tight knot formed in Michelle's stomach.

From her spot on the hill, Michelle could survey the entire lower pasture. And it wasn't empty. Mr. Montgomery was standing in the middle of the pasture, turning his head in every direction.

Quickly, Michelle ducked into the long grass. She didn't want Mr. Montgomery to see her. He might ask why she had wandered so far from the main stable. But she continued to stare at the bottom of the hill.

Now Mr. Montgomery was pacing in a circle and shaking his head back and forth.

Uh-oh. The lower pasture. That was where Annie had told her dad she had seen the foal. Mr. Montgomery was looking for Chestnut!

He wasn't alone, either. A man wearing a black cowboy hat was standing a few feet away from him, waving his arms and gazing around the pasture.

Hmmm . . . a cowboy hat? *The new owner!* Michelle realized in a flash. She had heard Mr. Montgomery tease the man about all his fancy cowboy hats. And the new owner *was* due at Sunset Farm anytime.

Michelle was positive she was right. The other man had come to take Chestnut to New York City!

Michelle's heart thudded in her chest. The men obviously realized Chestnut was missing. Any minute they were going to start a search.

Michelle ran the rest of the way back to the old barn.

I have to keep Chestnut safe just a little longer. Then Samantha Gilmore will call, and everything will be fine.

I hope.

Chapter
14

"I'm never coming back to this farm again," Stephanie murmured to herself. "After today, I never want to lay eyes on another horse."

After Jack told Stephanie to stay away from him, he had stalked off and disappeared into the stable. Stephanie could still feel the sting from his words.

Unfortunately, she couldn't simply leave Sunset Farm. She had promised Danny that she would stay until it was time for Michelle to go home.

Thank goodness Sabrina asked me to muck out a few more of these stables, Stephanie thought. It

105

wasn't the most glamorous job, but at least she could hide away in the stalls and keep anyone from noticing her.

There was no sign of Theresa today. At least that was a bit of good luck. Stephanie didn't think she could bear watching Jack tell the *real* girl of his dreams what a fool Stephanie was.

"Is this better, Montana?" Stephanie asked the horse standing next to her. "Are you going to be happy in your nice, clean stall?"

Okay. Maybe it wasn't true that Stephanie *never* wanted to see another horse. In fact, she was starting to enjoy the stable, regardless of everything that had happened with Jack.

"Stephanie, we need you out here!" Joe, the stable hand, called. He was standing in the open door of the barn, waving her over.

Stephanie's heart sank. Maybe Jack had told Mr. Montgomery she was the one who let Lightning out of her stall! Mr. Montgomery would probably give her a big lecture and make her feel even worse. Great. Just great.

Stephanie leaned the pitchfork she was using against the wall. Before she left, she made double sure that the latch on Montana's stall was hooked. A repeat episode of Lightning's freak-out would be totally awful.

Joe pointed to a large group assembled next to the corral. "Mr. M. wants to talk to all of us about something," Joe explained.

"Oh." Stephanie sighed.

"I need everyone's attention!" Mr. Montgomery shouted. "We seem to have a situation on our hands."

Stephanie stood at the edge of the group, surveying the scene. Standing next to Mr. Montgomery was a man Stephanie had never seen before. He wore a black cowboy hat, and he did *not* look happy. Whoever he was, he seemed to be having as bad a day as Stephanie.

"Has anyone seen Chestnut?" Mr. Montgomery asked the group.

People began murmuring to one another and shaking their heads.

"I took him out for some exercise yesterday afternoon," Sabrina called. "But I haven't seen him since."

Oh, no! Stephanie realized. Chestnut was missing!

She glanced around the group and spotted Cassie and Mandy. But where was Michelle?

Maybe she already knows Chestnut is missing, Stephanie guessed. If she does, she's probably off somewhere, really upset. Stephanie knew Chestnut was Michelle's all-time favorite horse.

I'll find her and see if she's okay as soon as I can, she decided. She hoped Michelle wasn't too crushed.

"Chestnut wasn't in his stall when I went to feed him this afternoon," Joe said. "I figured somebody had taken him out for a little fresh air."

Stephanie thought and thought. Had she seen Chestnut that afternoon? No. Definitely not.

Jack glanced at Stephanie from the other side of the group. "Maybe one of the volunteers accidentally lost him," he suggested to Mr. Montgomery.

"Did anyone lose Chestnut?" Mr. Montgomery asked. "If you did, speak up here and now."

The group was silent.

Mr. Montgomery shook his head. "I don't know what happened. But we *must* find that foal."

"I'll take the western trail," Jack offered. "Maybe Chestnut wandered over there."

"Thank you very much, Jack," Mr. Montgomery responded. "I know it's a lot to ask, but I need every one of you to help me locate Chestnut."

"I'll go south," Sabrina called. "My riding pupils and I will do a foot search of the pastures."

"I'll lead some of the volunteers in the wooded area to the north," Joe offered.

"Good. Good." Mr. Montgomery nodded as he jotted notes on a clipboard. "Thanks, everyone, for your help. This is a vital matter."

The group broke apart.

Stephanie wondered what she could do.

"Tim, Jack, and Stephanie, come with me," Joe called out.

"Wait!" Stephanie realized. "Shouldn't someone check the fences around the farm?" Stephanie asked Joe. "If one of them is broken, Chestnut could have slipped through."

"Good idea," Joe told her.

"Yeah," Jack chimed in. "I never would have thought of that."

"Stephanie, you take the fences. The boys and I will handle the wooded area," Joe instructed.

Stephanie nodded and headed off.

"I hope you find him," Mr. Montgomery called. "If that horse doesn't turn up inside of an hour, I'm going to call the police." He turned to the man beside him. "This is totally odd. I've never had a horse disappear."

Stephanie strode across the pastures toward the fence around the edge of the farm.

If I'm the one who finds Chestnut, Jack will have to realize that I'm not as clueless as he thinks, she decided. *Then even if he does already have a date for the dance, maybe we'll still have a chance at being friends.*

Stephanie studied the fence as she walked along, checking for broken rails. So far everything seemed intact.

She decided she would just keep walking until she found Chestnut.

Whew! She had no idea the farm was so big. In fact, it was huge. She checked her watch.

She'd been searching for at least an hour, and still no sign of Chestnut—or Michelle, for that matter.

Off to the left, Stephanie spotted an old barn.

Hmmm. I didn't know this was back here, she thought. Maybe I should check it out.

As Stephanie drew closer to the barn, she heard a soft noise coming from inside.

She stopped and held her breath, listening. There it was again! The noise sounded like . . . a whinny. Stephanie stared at the barn. Was it possible? Could Chestnut have somehow wandered inside?

She approached the barn and slid the door open. She took a few cautious steps inside—and gasped.

"Michelle!" Stephanie stared at her little sister in shock. "What are you doing in here?"

Wait a minute, Stephanie realized. Michelle wasn't alone. She was with—Chestnut!

MICHELLE

Chapter 15

As soon as the barn door opened, Michelle panicked.

Her mouth went totally dry and her stomach twisted into knots.

Then she realized it was only Stephanie.

Whew! Michelle's shoulders sagged with relief. For a second she thought she had actually been caught!

Stephanie grinned. "Everyone on this entire farm is searching for Chestnut—and you found him!"

"I guess I did find him. . . ." Michelle's voice trailed off. Stephanie didn't understand what was really going on. How was she going to explain?

"Come on!" Stephanie exclaimed. "Mr. Montgomery is going to be way psyched when he sees that we've got his horse."

"No!" Michelle cried. "We can't take him back. We have to keep Chestnut in here until Samantha Gilmore calls."

Stephanie frowned. "Michelle, you're not making any sense. Who is Samantha Gilmore? What are you talking about?"

This was it, Michelle realized. She had to spill her guts to her sister.

"If we bring Chestnut back, the man in the black cowboy hat is going to take him to New York City and make him pull a carriage," she said.

"What?" Stephanie asked, her voice full of surprise. "I hadn't heard anything about that. Are you sure?" Stephanie walked over to Chestnut and tenderly petted the foal.

"I'm positive. I've spent all week trying to find a way to save Chestnut! I thought I had everything figured out, but now my whole plan is falling apart." Michelle felt as if she couldn't get the words out fast enough.

"Hold on, Michelle," Stephanie interrupted. "Start from the beginning."

Michelle sighed. "Annie told me that her dad is selling Clancy and Chestnut. And we found out that a man from New York is buying them!" She paused to let that horrible piece of information sink in.

Stephanie nodded. "Go on."

"Chestnut *can't* get shipped off to New York City. He's too young and way too small to survive as a carriage horse in Central Park," Michelle explained.

Stephanie was nodding—a good sign. "But what can you do to stop it?" she asked. "You can't hide the horse in here forever."

"I know! That's why I talked to Samantha Gilmore at the San Francisco Zoo. The new petting zoo doesn't have a horse yet—and she promised to talk to Mr. Montgomery about buying Chestnut."

"But the man who's buying him is already here," Stephanie pointed out. "It's too late."

Michelle edged closer to Chestnut and put

her arms around the foal's neck. "Don't say that. As long as Chestnut is *here* instead of *there*, he has a chance."

"Michelle . . ." Stephanie was using her big sister voice. "We have to bring Chestnut back."

Michelle wasn't giving up on Chestnut— and that was that!

"Look at Chestnut!" Michelle pointed to the horse. "Do you want to go to New York City someday and see him pulling some heavy carriage through the traffic?"

"Of course not," Stephanie answered. "But, Michelle, the horse doesn't belong to us. He belongs to Mr. Montgomery. We can't stop him from selling his own foal!"

"He still can," Michelle insisted. "We just have to make sure he sells Chestnut to the petting zoo."

Stephanie stared at Chestnut. Michelle knew that her sister had a big heart. She wouldn't want to see the horse get hurt. But she also wouldn't want to get in trouble. Would she agree to keep Chestnut hidden from the man in the black cowboy hat?

"Please!" Michelle begged. "Think about Chestnut, Steph."

"Stephanie!" a boy's voice called, breaking the silence. "I decided to come along and check the fences with you. Are you in here? Is everything okay?"

Michelle recognized the voice. It belonged to Jack.

Her heart sank. Jack was the only reason Stephanie was even there. She didn't care about horses as much as Michelle did—she just wanted to impress the boy she had a crush on. Finding Chestnut would probably be a great way to do it.

Michelle closed her eyes. Would her own sister rat her out?

Chapter
16

Stephanie stood silent for a moment, trying to decide which was the right thing to do. Tell Jack what was going on or keep quiet?

She walked to the back door of the barn and peeked out. "Uh—hi, Jack. Everything's fine. There's nothing in here."

Jack sighed. "Well, I'm going to keep searching along the fence—and so should you."

"Right. I'll, um, be right there," Stephanie said quickly.

Stephanie shook her head as Jack walked away. Finding Chestnut would have totally impressed him, but Stephanie couldn't bring herself to betray her little sister.

Especially when Chestnut meant so much to Michelle.

Besides, Michelle was right. New York City was a terrible place for a horse—especially one as tiny and delicate as Chestnut.

"Thank you, Stephanie." Michelle smiled. "You're really the greatest."

Stephanie shrugged. "What's a sister for?"

"There's just one thing I didn't tell you about," Michelle said softly.

"What is it?" Stephanie demanded.

"I think Chestnut is sick," Michelle said. "Annie and I looked at a veterinary book to try to figure out what was wrong with him, but we couldn't."

Stephanie stared more closely at the little foal. She hadn't spent nearly as much time with him as Michelle had, but she had to agree. He didn't look very good. In fact, he looked kind of . . . sad.

"He won't eat *anything*," Michelle added. "And his eyes aren't as bright as they usually are. That can't be good."

Stephanie nodded. She hadn't noticed it before, but there were two whole buckets of oats in Chestnut's makeshift stall. There was even a bunch of carrots lying on the floor. She didn't know a lot about horses—but she knew they usually inhaled carrots.

"Has Chestnut been this way for long?" Stephanie asked.

"He was fine when we brought him here yesterday—while everyone was trying to help Jack get loose from Amazon."

Stephanie's face burned at *that* memory. But there were more important things to focus on.

"You just said 'we brought him here.' Who helped you, Michelle?" Stephanie asked.

"Mandy, Cassie, and Annie." Michelle stared mournfully at the small colt. She looked as if she were about to lose her best friend.

Stephanie sighed deeply. Michelle loved Chestnut so much, but deep down Stephanie knew what had to be done.

"We have to tell someone what's going on," Stephanie declared. "It's the only way to make sure that Chestnut isn't really sick—and that he's going to be okay."

A tear slid down Michelle's cheek. "Who can we tell?" she asked. "Everyone on the farm wants to *find* Chestnut so they can ship him to New York City. They're not going to help us hide him."

"I'm going to get Jack," Stephanie decided out loud.

"No way! Jack will want to take Chestnut back to Mr. Montgomery!" Michelle cried. "He's going to give him to the new owner!"

"Maybe," Stephanie agreed. "But maybe not. Jack loves horses more than anything in the world. I don't think he knows Chestnut and Clancy are set to move to New York City. He wouldn't want Chestnut to go through life pulling a heavy carriage any more than you do, Michelle. If we explain the whole situation to him, maybe he'll see things our way."

Michelle put a hand on Chestnut's soft mane of brown hair. "No matter what Jack says, you won't let anything bad happen to Chestnut, will you?"

"I'll do everything I can to help him," Stephanie promised.

Michelle nodded. "Okay. Jack is a nice person. I think he'll understand."

Stephanie smiled. "So do I," she assured her sister.

But inside, Stephanie wasn't as confident as Michelle. Jack was a very honest person. He wasn't going to want to keep the truth from Mr. Montgomery.

She glanced at Michelle one more time, then headed toward the door to find Jack.

Chapter
17

I know you don't feel well right now," Michelle said to Chestnut. "But I'm positive that Jack will know how to make you better."

Michelle looked over her shoulder to make sure she was still alone. "Jack is really smart. That's one of the reasons Stephanie has such a major crush on him," she added in a loud whisper.

Stephanie had been gone for almost five minutes. What was taking so long? Michelle bit her lip, studying Chestnut's sad face. Her horse needed help—now!

Michelle heard voices outside the barn. "It's

122

them," Michelle told Chestnut. "Now be good."

I hope we did the right thing, telling Jack about our plan, Michelle worried.

The wooden door opened. Stephanie's and Jack's faces blocked the late afternoon sun. Michelle stepped away from Chestnut, her heart beating fast. This was the moment of truth.

"I'm confused, Stephanie," Jack was saying. "I thought you said Chestnut wasn't in here."

"Michelle will explain everything to you," Stephanie promised him. She walked into the barn. "Won't you, Michelle?"

"It's not Stephanie's fault," Michelle said quickly. "Really. It was all my idea."

Jack shook his head as he approached the horse. "What? What was your idea? I still don't understand."

"We'll tell you everything," Michelle said. "But first you have to examine Chestnut." She gestured toward the little colt. "He's sick."

Instantly, concern shadowed Jack's face. He knelt by Chestnut's side. "I'll look at him," he told Michelle. "While I do that, you tell me what's going on."

"Tell him," Stephanie urged.

Michelle's eyes brimmed with tears as she started her story. "Mr. Montgomery is going to sell Chestnut and Clancy to that man in the cowboy hat," she began. "And he's going to take them to New York City!"

Jack frowned. "New York *City?* Are you sure?"

Michelle nodded her head vigorously. "I heard him talking about it on the phone. I'm *positive.*"

"Michelle knows a woman at the San Francisco Zoo," Stephanie told Jack. "She thinks this woman can buy Chestnut and give him a home in the new petting zoo instead."

"It'll be a million times better for him," Michelle said. "He's too little to work in New York City."

"Now do you see?" Stephanie asked Jack. "Michelle was just trying to protect Chestnut."

Jack stared into Chestnut's eyes. He nodded. "I can tell you really care about this horse," he said softly.

Michelle felt a smile creep across her face. "I do, Jack! I do!" She felt a flicker of hope.

"And I know you want what is best for him." Now Jack turned away from Chestnut and gazed into Michelle's eyes.

"Of course," Michelle agreed. "And that means hiding him from Mr. Montgomery until it's time for him to go to the petting zoo."

Jack shook his head. "Michelle, Chestnut isn't sick—not the way you think he is."

"What do you mean?" Michelle didn't like the tone in Jack's voice. He sounded as if he were about to deliver bad news.

"Chestnut doesn't have a cold or anything like that," Jack explained. "It's just that little horses need to be near their mothers. Chestnut is terribly, terribly lonely without Clancy."

Michelle glanced at Stephanie, then back at Jack. "That's why he won't eat or drink anything?"

Jack nodded. "A baby horse needs to be with his mother," he repeated. "Kind of like human babies."

Michelle thought about her little twin cousins, Nicky and Alex. They hated to be far from Aunt Becky for very long, and they were even older than Chestnut.

"Well—maybe we can get Samantha to buy Clancy, too," Michelle suggested. "Clancy would be a great horse for a petting zoo."

Jack stood up and patted Chestnut's side. "We can ask Mr. Montgomery about that later," he agreed. "But right now we need to take Chestnut back to his mother."

Michelle sighed. There was a huge lump in her throat, but she wasn't going to let herself cry. She had to be strong—for Chestnut. "I understand," she whispered softly.

She walked to Chestnut's side and put her arms around the foal. "I'm sorry, Chestnut. I tried . . ."

Stephanie, Jack, and Michelle were silent as they led Chestnut out of the old barn and began the long walk back to Sunset Farm's main stable. Michelle knew deep down that Jack was right about Chestnut. She felt sick every time she thought of Chestnut being shipped off to New York, anyway.

It just wasn't fair!

Jack squeezed Michelle's shoulder as they neared the stable. In the distance Michelle could see Mr. Montgomery pacing back and forth in front of the corral.

Mr. Montgomery and the man in the cowboy hat spotted Stephanie, Michelle, Jack, and Chestnut. They rushed toward the group with huge smiles on their faces.

"You found him!" Mr. Montgomery shouted. "Good job, kids! I knew you could do it!"

As soon as he was close enough, Mr. Montgomery reached out and shook Jack's hand, then Stephanie's. But when he got to Michelle, she left her hand at her side.

"I didn't find Chestnut," she told the stable owner. "I've known where he was all along."

Mr. Montgomery frowned. "What do you mean?"

"I hid him in the abandoned barn," Michelle confessed, her voice wavering.

"But why?" Mr. Montgomery asked. "Michelle, why would you ever do such a thing?"

"Because Michelle didn't want Chestnut to have a horrible life in New York City," Annie Montgomery called out.

She jogged toward them. Cassie and

Mandy were close behind. All the girls looked worried.

Michelle groaned. She wished she hadn't dragged her friends into her mission to save Chestnut. Now they were *all* going to get into trouble.

"What are you saying, Annie?" Mr. Montgomery demanded. "Did you have a part in this?"

"Annie was just trying to help me," Michelle said. "I thought Chestnut was too small to lug around a carriage full of tourists like those horses in New York City do, so I convinced her to help me hide him."

"Just until we got a hold of the lady from the petting zoo," Cassie piped up. "The lady who promised to adopt Chestnut."

"That's where Chestnut belongs," Mandy added. "New York City is no place for a horse."

Mr. Montgomery blinked several times. "None of you is making an ounce of sense," he said. "Can someone please explain this craziness?"

The man in the cowboy hat stepped forward. "Hold on a second," he told Mr. Montgomery. "Let me see if I can't get to the bottom of this."

"By all means," Mr. Montgomery said. "I'm completely lost."

"My name is Roger Rollins," the man said to the small group. "And if I've got this straight, you kids think I'm about to haul your favorite horses off to New York City."

"You *are!*" Michelle blurted out. "I heard Mr. Montgomery talking about it on the telephone."

Mr. Rollins shook his head. "I think we have a little misunderstanding here, young lady. I *am* taking the horses to New York," he admitted. "But not to New York City!"

"What?" Annie asked. "But we thought— we thought you were going to turn Chestnut into one of those carriage horses for tourists!"

Mr. Rollins laughed. "I live on a great big farm in upstate New York, where there's grass and trees as far as the eye can see. I've got all kinds of animals on my farm there—including horses."

"But what about the heavy carriages?" Mandy asked. "Do you have any of those?"

"Nope. Not a one. And I'm not going to make these fine animals toil away in the pollution of the Big Apple. I'm going to set them free on my farm."

"Where they will be very happy," Mr. Montgomery added. "Mr. Rollins has one of the most beautiful spreads in the whole country."

Oops. A horrible realization dawned on Michelle. She *had* heard Mr. Montgomery speaking of New York. But he never specifically mentioned New York *City*. Michelle had filled that part in herself.

Nobody ever planned to make Chestnut work as a carriage horse in Central Park. She had been wrong. Totally, completely, one hundred percent *wrong*.

Michelle took a small step forward and cleared her throat.

"I'm really, truly sorry that I caused so much trouble," Michelle said to Mr. Montgomery and Mr. Rollins. "I didn't mean to do anything wrong. I was just trying to help Chestnut."

Mr. Rollins grinned and tipped his cowboy hat. "Don't you worry about it. Helping a horse is a noble deed."

"Is Annie in trouble?" Michelle asked Mr. Montgomery.

He shook his head. "On this one, I'll have to agree with Roger." He gestured to the man in the cowboy hat. "I taught my daughter to care about animals. Today she proved that she does."

Mr. Montgomery led Chestnut through the stable and into her stall. In the very next stall, Clancy stood waiting.

A huge whinny escaped Chestnut when he caught sight of his mother. Clancy shook her head and nickered in response.

When Chestnut was carefully locked in, Clancy leaned her head over the rail separating the two horses and touched Chestnut's nose with her own.

At that moment, Michelle thought, the sparkle magically returned to Chestnut's eyes. He nuzzled his mother for a moment, then leaned down to crunch on a carrot.

Mr. Montgomery patted Michelle on the shoulder. "Chestnut just needs a little tender loving care from his mother, and he'll be as good as new."

"Really?" Michelle asked.

"Yep." Mr. Montgomery smiled. "Michelle, we know you did what you did because you love Chestnut. That's the important thing."

Michelle felt happier than she had in days. Clancy and Chestnut were going to have a wonderful home after all. A horse farm would be an even better place for them than the petting zoo.

Michelle closed her eyes. She pictured the horse running across a wide-open field, his shiny mane blowing in the breeze. Yes, he was going to be happy, which meant that everything was okay.

Except for one thing. Michelle was still going to have to find a way to say good-bye to her favorite foal.

STEPHANIE

Chapter
18

Stephanie grinned to herself. Michelle talked to horses as if they were people. And the crazy thing was that the horses seemed to *understand.*

"Thanks for helping me learn to ride," Michelle said to Clancy the next afternoon. "Without you, I wouldn't be ready to try jumping so soon."

Then Michelle nuzzled her face against Chestnut's. The foal shook his head and whinnied—just the way he had before he started to miss his mother so much.

"I know you're worried about the winters

in New York," she told the colt. "But Mr. Montgomery and my dad both told me all about how beautiful upstate New York is."

She gave the young horse a kiss. "I know you're going to love it there. Maybe we'll even come and visit you someday."

Stephanie giggled. "Stranger things have happened in the Tanner family," she told Michelle—and Chestnut.

Stephanie watched as Michelle gave Chestnut one last hug. The little foal and Clancy were about to start their long journey to New York.

Michelle turned away, and Chestnut was loaded onto a special trailer.

"Are you all right?" Stephanie asked her little sister.

Michelle smiled. "I'm sad to say good-bye to Chestnut and Clancy," she said. "But I'm happy that they're both going to have such a nice home."

Stephanie nodded. "I'm proud of you, Michelle. I know how much you would love to have Clancy and Chestnut nearby."

Stephanie gazed at her little sister. "But,

hey! Thanks to you, I found a new place that I really love—this stable."

Michelle frowned. "Really?"

"Sure. I mean, I started volunteer work at the farm mostly because I was hoping to get a date to the dance. But now I really *like* being here. Jack or no Jack."

"Hey, Michelle. Did you get to say your good-byes?" Jack asked.

Whoops! Stephanie hadn't heard Jack approach. She hoped he hadn't heard any of their conversation.

"Yes, I did. Thanks for all of your help, Jack." Michelle smiled shyly. "You were right about Chestnut. Now that he's back with his mother, he looks better than ever."

Jack turned to Stephanie. "Hey. I, uh, wanted to tell you I'm sorry," he began.

"I think I hear Cassie and Mandy calling me," Michelle interrupted. "See you later." She turned and tore off toward the barn.

Stephanie smiled. Cute. Michelle thought she was giving Stephanie and Jack some private time together. Too bad it wouldn't amount to anything.

"I'm sorry I got so angry with you the other day," Jack started again. "I know you were just trying to be nice."

"Please!" Stephanie exclaimed. "You had every right to be mad. I nearly got you killed."

"Also, it was really nice of you—the way you handled that situation with your sister and Chestnut," Jack pointed out.

Stephanie blushed. "Well, you know. We're sisters. We take care of each other."

"I know, it's like when Theresa and I don't see eye to eye about things . . ."

Stephanie stopped short.

Wait a minute. What did Jack just say?

"You should see the way we fight at home," he continued. "It drives our mom crazy."

"Theresa," Stephanie asked, "is your *sister?*"

Jack nodded. "Yeah. I thought you knew that."

Stephanie laughed out loud. All this time she had been worried about Jack and Theresa being a couple. And they *were* a couple—of siblings! How could she have been so silly?

Jack frowned. "Stephanie? What are you laughing at?"

"It's just—I just can't believe—" Stephanie cleared her throat. "Jack, would you like to go to the dance with me next week?"

Jack stared at her, his eyes wide. "Really?" he asked. "You're asking me to the dance?"

This time he started laughing.

"I guess I'll take that as a no," Stephanie muttered.

"No! I mean yes!" Jack yelled. "I mean, sure I'll go to the dance with you. It's just that—I was about to ask you to go with me!"

"Wow!" Stephanie gasped. "This is awesome!" She felt a huge smile spread across her face. She'd gotten her dream date to the dance after all. Even if it wasn't quite the way she'd planned to do it.

Michelle appeared in the door of the barn. "Come on, guys!" she called. "We're putting together a carrot-care-package for Chestnut and Clancy."

Stephanie felt Jack's warm hand wrap around hers. "Come on. Might as well help out," he said.

They walked into the barn, grinning from ear to ear.

All right! she thought. *Now Jack and I can ride off into the sunset together, after all. . . .*

Michelle gazed at her and Jack. A big smile spread across her face as she noticed their hands clasped together.

Michelle grabbed a carrot, then handed one to her sister. "To Chestnut," Michelle toasted. "May he always have carrots to munch on."

"To sisters," Stephanie stated. "Where would we be without them?"